For my gorgeous star, Oona Balloona.

table of contents

broken head

There is that fear in saying things. Not just command of the language – the proper words, the stomachache of locution – but also the subjecting pressure of meaning, of making sense, of having something to *say*. And even then there is the danger of spitting in the wrong direction. Factual errors are like misplaced zeros: a basic problem of diminishing returns on your verbal investment. Compounded, it can adversely affect your entire bottom line (unless you surround yourself with the similarly bankrupt, whistling away your days on an illiterate Baltic Avenue). Still, the world is a complicated place, rattling with loose noise; mistakes happen, and are gleefully expected. The real peril is the power to offend and inflict, where kissed words are hissed sparks, and lo and behold behind the red curtain there is only the stunning failure of internal machinery, the teeth of contraption exposed, that embarrassing broken-down spectacle of affliction and grief.

This is the kind of shit I don't worry about anymore. The accident changed all that.

The dedication which follows – written for the original hardcover edition of *Broken Head* – was approved without the slightest argument from my then editor. Not a single, delicate, wincing word. Surprising the hell out of me. I enjoyed, by virtue of my track record, I guess, a certain amount of latitude. Or maybe he just wanted to be different (for those prancing literary parties – *Did you take a boo at the dedication?* – glass raised to lips, simpering smile) or the book to be remarkable (singular in its poisonousness), spinning for market, stories within stories and blood everywhere, the twisty bastard.

Nevertheless. Four books into it and I could finally name names. *Fine*, I thought.

For Seline, raven-haired and thin but with hips and perfectly pointed breasts, who agreed to marry me strictly on the basis of my dedication to her, my shameless worship of her, and against the advice of her destitute but judicious parents, who quite correctly surmised that my career prospects were necessarily limited by the lack of corporate consciousness down at the lumberyard, not to mention my complete and obvious inability to grasp abstract concepts. *Goddamn that boy is dense!* I heard her mother sing more than once. Still, we had my uncle's trailer, that big yard and those sundresses that let the light through. Stagey circles beneath your shaded eyes. I miss you.

For Jack Lamb, who used to be on my paper route as a kid, a great tipper at Christmas and always with a joke the rest of the year (although I didn't really receive about half of them, just waiting until the end to show my teeth). Who got me that job at the lumberyard, who helped put food on our tiny table. *Don't thank me, I'm taking ten percent off the top*, he laughed. Who knew when I was working – dropping in for a bag of nails just to make sure – and then around to see the wife. A small town and all that, very sociable. Who acted the way he was hard-wired to, everyone knew the stories (I found out later).

For the guys down at the Cambridge Hotel, a real Society of Friends (without the burdensome opposition to violence), who told me stories, these beer-stained things that I didn't need to hear. Advocates of courage, or at least vigorous promoters of *what a guy should do*.

For the fine work of Doctor Warner, who not three weeks before had corrected my vision with glasses that I actually liked, no more Coke bottles, tremendously effective for seeing Jack and Seline clearly after bursting in, no mistaking it, not even in the dim light at the back of that trailer, God how I used to love that little bedroom. The searing thought of it now, her thighs so white.

For my dad, who always stormed out instead of hitting my mom. It sticks in a kid's memory, the sound of that truck door slamming, the growl of crushed gravel, although you don't realize it until you're spinning tire wheels in your own yard all those years later. The slow thought finally trickling through.

For Charlie Mason, who lived as people thought he would – and should. Every town needs a drunk, true to the character of his degenerate personality and rusted pick-up, right through that stop sign, didn't even see the fucker. Whenever I'm back there I go piss on his grave.

For a certain major automobile manufacturer, be proud of your product, especially the steering wheel that doesn't break upon impact with a human skull.

For God and the mystery of his engines.

For the doctors who didn't think I'd come through, *comatose* they said, just the look on their faces when I opened my eyes and talked back that day, like a spark in their heads, never mind with a voice that spoke the terms of their language better than they did. Or, at least after I got my hands on a medical dictionary. One man's brain injury, another man's awakening.

And what a fine thing it is to understand, aside from the occasional headaches.

red horse leader

0)

In a factory in the south of China, a line worker named Zhi Chen inspects a toy figurine. The figurine is two inches tall, plastic, with an oval base. It is a tiny red horse. The figurine is meant to depict the horse running wild; its muscles strain and its eyes bulge accordingly. On the underside of the base are the words RED HORSE LEADER and MUCH LUCK. If questioned, the line worker would say he is satisfied with the product (this is, after all, only a random and cursory exercise in quality control). He tosses the figurine into a box with hundreds of others. Thousands of these boxes leave the factory every day. They go all around the world.

The line worker has the beginnings of a black cloud in his brain. For now he only has headaches. Within a year he will lose the capacity to distinguish the weather in his brain from the weather outside his window. A year after that he'll be dead.

1)

Scratched. That's what they called it when a horse didn't make it to the race. They'd announce it over the loudspeakers: *Ladies and gentlemen, we have a change for the upcoming race. Please scratch number five, RunChumRun, from your racing programs and handicap sheets. Number five, RunChumRun, is a scratch.* Most people just drew a line through the horse's name but Greg liked to scribble right over it, literally scratch it out. It felt more finished that way, like that horse didn't matter at all anymore.

You could do that with people, too. Just make a list. It couldn't be too long though: any list was weakest at its end. You had to forget about high school and old jobs and just stick with the situation at hand, what you had to do now and who deserved it. The line had to be drawn somewhere. It was a pyramid of need.

Heather was not on the list. Adele was. What happened wasn't Heather's fault. It was Adele's. One day Greg was married and then he wasn't. Question: what changed in the meantime? Answer: Adele came along. No way Heather would leave him if it wasn't for Adele. Heather wouldn't get that kind of idea on her own, that wasn't the girl he married, not at all. They were happy. They were a normal, happy couple. There was never any trouble until Heather met Adele. Adele was the one who wrecked everything. Adele was the one who came between them. Even when he went down on his knees to beg her not to go, all Heather could do was bring up Adele: *Adele says I don't have to live like this, Adele says I have the right to be happy, to have a future.* It always came back to Adele. Adele poisoned Heather's mind against him. And why did Adele do this? Because that bitch was never going to get married, couldn't hang on to a man so of course she told Heather all kinds of shit, it was all just a game to her, she had to wreck it for everybody. Anyway, Adele was at the top of the list, SCRATCH NUMBER ONE.

It was not gambling, gambling was not the problem, it was Adele.

Greg chewed on a plastic figurine. His nephew had left it in Greg's truck one day, this little red horse, and he took it as a sign that he should switch from football games to the races. It had been his good luck charm ever since. He liked to chew on it while he tried to think.

Maybe today, if he had any luck, he would go buy that Glock.

Maybe today, if he didn't have any luck, he would go deal with the neighbour's dog, who was also on the list, just begging to be scratched.

2)

It was the weekend and Adele was hiding. She unplugged the phone, went to soak in the tub. She was sick of counselling Heather. Heather acted like the end of her marriage was the end of the world. *Quit crying about it*, Adele told her. *It's getting boring.*

Adele had her own problems. They bored her almost as much. Sometimes she would try to visualize them, the actual words, like a marquee in her head:

> *Bad job*
> *No boyfriend*
> *Dad going crazy*
> *Now Playing*
> *Adele Morel*

Adele arranged a washcloth over her face, closed her eyes, inhaled the warm wetness, thought about the safety of hidden places. Her mind went still for almost a minute. Maybe she could wish it all away. Then she thought about her dad and his dark house and his thousands of figurines, on every possible surface, crushed together like passengers on the deck of a sinking ship.

3)

Everything was poisoned by the numbers of the Beast. Soon there would be a False Christ in the White House. And then? The Apocalypse, stupid!

Adele's father knew exactly what to do: buy more plastic horses. Then there would be no room for the Four Horsemen.

What made him weep late at night was that there was no way to save all his foster children in Africa: Zalika, Nabila, Binah, Binta, Habika, Kadija, Kapera, Caimile, and Faizah. Everyone knew that Africa was the beginning and the end of the circle.

4)

Faizah did not understand. One minute she was playing *jolis chevaux* and the next everything went crazy, the smoke and the screams and the people getting shot in the neck, bursting like spit. What changed? The soldiers of Red Leader came. Now the village was burning. Mamma grabbed her hand so hard it hurt, dragged her running into the bush. *We have to reach the bridge*, she cried. *We have to reach the bridge.* Why was this happening? Faizah prayed at the church every Sunday, prayed with her eyes closed tight and sang all the good Christian songs loud and clear to the coming of the Lord. *Je t'aime, Jesus! Amen!* Faizah loved Jesus with all her heart, dreamed about him all the time. Jesus with his blue eyes was so beautiful! But why didn't Jesus protect them from the evil soldiers? Why didn't Jesus come down and strike the soldiers dead? Perhaps God would not let him. Perhaps God said, *No Jesus, their fiery pit is not ready yet, I have not made arrangements with the Devil, they are not on the list, not yet.* This was not fair. Just because God was not properly organized, she and Mamma had to run for their lives. There would be no hot supper tonight. Yet deep down Faizah knew she could not blame God for this because doing so would be a sin. Jesus would save them. He would deal with the evil soldiers and put Red Leader in a cage, even if it took awhile. She kept running.

5)

Red Leader wants to get it right this time. He wants to express himself clearly. He wants to properly convey the immensity of his message. He wants his words to be a force, to reveal themselves as a dragon in descent, lungs afire, the serpent sent from heaven, then transformed. He wants to demonstrate his abilities, his gift, his special knowledge. *Tomorrow will be a bad day for the false prophets*, he says, smiling at this young Canadian journalist by his side.

The journalist struggles along in his notepad, his fingers cramping. He doesn't want to miss a single word. The journalist sees his entire career in the black ink of his cursive, the whole of his professional life staked on this moment. For over two years he has treated himself badly, put himself in harm's way, risked middle-of-the-night meetings in bottomless places, damp blindfolds and pistols pressed hard to his head, *death instinct* he heard in his mind's wilderness more than once before finally being granted this precious interview, this distant light in the rain. The journalist knows of at least three men who have gone before him, who folded themselves into the trunks of cars and were never seen again. Still, all he can think is: *two hours access, two hours of quotes from the scariest guy on the planet*. It is the journalistic achievement of a lifetime. It is calls from magazines around the world, the guest chair beside the national news anchor, the book deal and American money and beautiful German women at parties in London.

All he has to do is make it out of here alive. *Soon*, he hears Red Leader say, *some people will pay dearly for their beliefs*.

The two walk as Red Leader talks. Twelve men follow a few paces behind, careful not to come too close. They bump into each other like badly played ghosts, jingling and clinking from layers of beads, trinkets, jewellery, ammunition belts. Their AK-47s are a mess of dirt and thick rust in the grooves. Their clothes are a bewildering mix of track shorts and sneakers, trench coats and life jackets, denim skirts and sequined prom dresses, halter tops and long, blonde wigs. One man has a yellow happy-face painted on his forehead. His skin shines like an open barrel of oil.

Red Leader stops at a high vantage point. In a script the scene arranged on the plateau below could be called SECRET BASE FOR SECRET, AVENGING ARMY. Today it has been staged for maximum menace. Everywhere there are frantic stick-figures rushing around crude obstacle courses, training with rocket launchers, mortars and automatic weapons. Women shoot pistols at department-store mannequins. A group of children does a dancing sort of drill with flags, gleefully singing out praise to *Red Leader the Father, Oo-ooh the Great Father.* Greasy tails of smoke make the landscape seem to drift. In the distance is a row of crucifixes. *There is a famous picture,* Red Leader continues, *of Japanese pilots in the mess hall of one of the aircraft carriers headed for Pearl Harbour, laughing as they listen to a radio broadcast from Honolulu. Do you know it?*

The journalist looks up from his pen, blinks, nods, then averts his eyes again.

Despite the spectacular thing we do tomorrow, ours is not that kind of extravagance, not that kind of hollow joy. As instruments of salvation we feel only the calming rapture of God's infinite love. Red Leader raises a finger to underscore his point. *It is the resolve that cannot be defeated.* He sits down on a large flat rock, strokes a tattoo of a weeping cross on the side of his face, squints under the afternoon sun. On a chain around his neck he wears a plastic figurine, a little red horse with teeth marks.

The journalist stands beside him, steals little looks while making side notes in shorthand.

The Red Army of God wages war with a world corrupted. For this, Red Leader is hunted and persecuted by the agents of the Beast. The government gets help from the French and the Americans. Who helps us? All we have is the faith, and the love, and that remains unshakable. And ye shall be hated of all men for my name's sake: but he that shall endure unto the end, the same shall be saved.

Red Leader motions for the young Canadian journalist to sit on the stony ground. *Jesus threatened the powers of his time, institutions that broke the spirit of the common man. What happened just before the crucifixion? Jesus threw the money-changers out of the temple. The money-changers were bad men; they made indecent profits from pilgrims to the temple. Jesus made a whip of cords and drove them out, with the sheep and the oxen, and spilled the changers' money and ·*

*overturned their tables. He called it a den of thieves and said
to those who sold doves, Take these things away! Do not make
my father's house a house of merchandise! He foretold the de-
struction of the temple. Seest thou these great buildings?
There shall not be left one stone upon another, that shall not
be thrown down. Do you know what happened?*

The journalist clears his throat. *The Romans came and
burned it.*

Red Leader is visibly pleased. *That's right. The legions of
Rome marched forth and the words of Jesus were fulfilled.
The Romans acted with great cruelty, eviscerating the
women and children who tried to hide gold coins by swallowing them. The Roman general Titus set aside two thousand captives to be burned alive or fed to wild animals at
the festival games for his brother's birthday. These were the
rewards of the money-lenders' sin. And so it shall be when
the Red Army of God overthrows the same institutions that
want to subjugate the people with filthy lucre.* Red Leader
sighs, slowly drums his fingers on his forehead. Distant ex-
plosions go *caawumpwump* in the surrounding hills.

*It is sad that so many of my children will die tomorrow,
when we make our assault to liquidate the parliament. It is
the price they pay for salvation. Only the truly righteous
have the bulletproof, you see. If they have the faith then they
have the bulletproof. All doubters will surely perish. This is
the will of God, who forgives them in heaven. We cannot feel
sorry for them. We cannot waver from our course. The parliament must be liquidated. The altar of Mammon must be
destroyed. It suffers from the dementia of money and we are
the cure. There are many so afflicted in the parasitic city. The
government exercises social and economic injustice, it deals
in human souls. It will be wiped clean with blood, their ruth-
less malfeasance put to an end. The treacherous dealers have
dealt treacherously; yea, the treacherous dealers have dealt
very treacherously. The only true currency is the bond of
God.*

The journalist can sense Red Leader study him as he writes. His scalp itches. A finger flickers up to a bruise at his temple, feels the broken skin before falling again. Above his head the sky is milky like bathwater. *Can I tell you something, young man?* he hears Red Leader ask him. The tone is almost confidential. The journalist says nothing, pretends the only thing he can move is his hand around his pen.

I love being Red Leader. Red Leader is pure. Red Leader is love. Red Leader is living in God's grace. It is a trust, you see. When I look down on my children my heart swells a thousand times over. In the eyes of this army is the soul of my every word. They are an instrument of my best ambition. To hear the simple words ... Yes, Red Leader ... that is everything. I am special and blessed. Red Leader is all. What else is there? Red Leader hums, almost moans, runs his hand across his mouth. *Yet mine is a terrible responsibility. My army is also my own sin before me. No man is without guilt. I do not do any of this lightly. No one can judge me.*

Red Leader goes silent for a full minute, then suddenly stands up. A big breath comes out of him like a man finishing a glass of water. The interview is over. *This went much better than the other ones*, he announces. He looks over to the twelve men. *Don't you agree?*

The men all nod, rattle, murmur softly.

The journalist remains sitting, scribbling away in Red Leader's shadow. He knows he is taking too long, suddenly thinks of a damp prairie morning, a long-ago English exam pulled from his grasp, the sound of ripping paper.

Red Leader is shaking something, rattling something like dice in his cupped hands. With the flourish of a croupier he opens them, lets the pieces fall to the ground. They are little plastic figurines, like the one he wears around his neck. He leans over them, studying, cocks his head at their placement in the dirt. *Still*, Red Leader says, *it wasn't a perfect interview, was it? I don't see anything special here.*

The journalist stops writing. For the first time he feels a breeze across his lips. He hears the slow crunch of small stones behind him. Inside he feels something remembered, something deep and anxious, the child waiting for the doctor's needle, eyes squeezed to a sliver of light, the shudder suppressed. But he is not a child anymore.

Think of a number from one to ten, he blurts.

Red Leader looks startled. *What did you say?*

Think of a number from one to ten, the journalist repeats quickly. *But don't tell me.*

A grin seeps across Red Leader's face. *Oh, a game! You want to play a game! Okay young man, I am thinking of your number.* He makes a little motion like waving away a waiter.

The journalist senses the presence behind him retreat. For the first time he notices a skeleton in some bushes beside the path. It has no shoes but is wearing a blue Prada suit. *Good,* the journalist says, trying to smile. *Now multiply that number by nine.*

Red Leader flips his eyes in a small circle. *Yes.*

If the number is a two-digit number, then add the digits together.

Done.

Now subtract five.

Okay.

Now, determine which letter in the alphabet corresponds to that number. The number two would be the letter "b," for example.

Okay, yes, I understand.

Now think of a country that starts with that letter.

Yes.

Remember the last letter in the name of that country.

Yes, last letter.

Think of the name of an animal that starts with that letter.

Yes, an animal.

Remember the last letter in the name of that animal.

Yes, young man, I will remember.

Now, think of the name of a fruit that starts with that letter.

Yes.

The journalist looks Red Leader straight in the eye. *Are you thinking of a kangaroo in Denmark eating an orange?*

Red Leader blinks, does not make a sound but from the twelve men there are clattering whispers almost like laughter.

Ninety-nine percent of people come up with the same answer, the journalist says. Uncrossing his legs, unfolding himself, he rises to his feet in one smooth motion.

Red Leader shakes his head, turns his palms over skyward. *But I was not thinking of a kangaroo in Denmark, young man.*

Of course not, the Canadian journalist says, *you are Red Leader. Your name came from God.*

free rein

All Connor wanted was one big win. A grubby, material idea: he deserved it, he was due and how much he was due. Redemption's dollar figure. That was the spirit of the thing. Admittedly. But the idea had weight, the idea applied pressure. The idea held movement, momentum and more power than God this day, but he wanted to pray, needed to pray anyway and as he sat there, so precisely alone in the middle of the grandstand, he offered up the usual questions, the pleading and the hope. How much could a man lose? How long could the losing go on? The sweep of the flattened world before him, the racetrack in the oval of a snake eating its tail, contained its own intimations of infinity, while the washed and faded curtain of sky above played to thoughts of empty nets cast out to the vanity of open air, wishes like will-o-wisps, all those banked-upon souls long since spent into endless, needless silence.

His tenured friends would call this *influenced observation*.

As a professor of history Connor knew things, was supposed to know many things such as (for example) the mystical contents of the little book that Tojo required all Japanese soldiers to carry with them at all times, the little book with its loaded incantations like "Belief is power." Tojo the war criminal, the loser to be judged at the end of a rope. He could think of that and hold his head in his hands, could think of how losing made war against belief, how it scraped the soul hollow and turned the brain into a purple lump in the skull. But Connor could not think very well right now, had not been thinking very well for what seemed like a very long time. The length of his losing streak so very, very long.

Over sixty thousand dollars long. Clausewitz said war was never an isolated act. The jagged tip of the thing running ragged through his life. Connor could extend his palms in turn: here's to brink, here's to ruin. And God, he knew, would do nothing.

But give me something, Connor prayed.

As if on cue, Emma-O emerged from the mezzanine entrance just as the bugle sounded over the loudspeakers and the horses came out to parade for the fourth race, dancing in line with the trotters. For a twenty-year-old girl Emma-O had not the slightest hint of grace, moving heavily, dragging herself up the cement steps towards him. Tickets clutched in her left hand. On a day without sun she wore a sundress, her thick body blocked out in shadow against the immense grey light. She flashed him her lopsided smile, that same smile she showed when she sat with her legs open in public, her dress riding up, the flash crossing through air as the shame hit and surged through him. But she filled her tight dresses with the skin and flesh of a twenty-year-old girl, which made her, by the definition of his own age at fifty-two, beautiful. She groaned as she collapsed into the seat beside him. In one motion he dropped the racing form in her lap and threw her ridiculously small sweater over her shoulders.

"Tickets?" he asked, splaying his fingers.

"Here you go, mister," she smiled, placing the tickets with one hand and pinching him with the other. "I still think you should have bet on Saucy Vixen. Look she's a grey, too."

Connor checked the tickets before replying. "Well, that's one reason why I didn't. Another is that she's the favourite. Look at the board, your highness, she's three-to-two."

"Exactly," grinned Emma-O, pulling on his arm. "Everyone agrees with me!"

"Sweetheart, you don't understand odds. What's the point in betting just to make your money back?"

"At least you get to win ..." she said, before catching his return look and trailing off. She put on her sunglasses.

Connor had eight thousand dollars to bet this day, courtesy of the last of his children's savings bonds. It was the last of everything really, while still his wife knew nothing. Three races gone, six thousand dollars left. For the fourth race he liked a horse called Ma-mien, placing this horse at the centre of his wheeling exactor and triactor wagers. For the fourth race he bet a thousand dollars.

Ma-mien finished fourth, six-and-a-half lengths behind the winner, Saucy Vixen. Emma-O knew better than to say anything, simply pushed a bottom lip in Connor's direction and patted his thigh as he watched the horse prance and twist in the winner's enclosure.

In the fifth race Connor circled Amorite, remembering the passage in Joshua 10, the retreating army killed by hailstones sent from God for fighting the Israelites. Emma-O wrinkled her nose at the story. "Oh, I almost forgot," she said, squeezing around in her seat. "Some guy came up to me downstairs. He said his name was Danya, Danyo ... something like that? Anyway, he said he's some friend of yours and that him and some friends of his are gonna wait for us at the car after the races ...? Who is this guy anyway?"

"He's an exchange student," Connor lied. And kissed her.

"Mmm. I thought so, with a name like that. Creepy guy, though. Why doesn't he get his teeth fixed?"

"You should do your sweater up," Connor said, not looking at her. "It's getting cooler."

Emma-O made an unseen face. "Why can't we go inside, where it's warm?"

"Because I like to watch the races."

"You can watch on the TV screens."

"It's not the same. Do your sweater up."

The fifth race didn't take very long, a horse called Dead Quick surging away from the start, blowing out the field. "Sorry Connor-Cruise," Emma-O said. She called him

Connor-Cruise after an author's name she had heard at university, a political science writer named Connor Cruise O'Brien. She loved that name, her imagined elegance in it. In fact Connor's father had chosen his name along the same thematic grounds, said it was a solid name for a gentleman. His father, an elegant man in his own right, so contained in the sheen of black cloth, so distinguished by his collar. The grace of his movements, those grazing tips of fingers from the back of his hand, the flicking lick and snack of his belt that spun, as if charmed, in whirls over his head. Connor could remember it in frames, the liquefied click of freezing seconds, like stop-action photography, bodies composed by motion. *There's no salvation in running boy!* and here the mind spins faster than the body, and the feet have no thought.

For the sixth race, the second last, his chest tightening, Connor forced himself to like a jet-black horse called Izanami. For once it was handicapped, one of the three favourites for the race. He bet a thousand dollars. The surprise winner was Last Lady Luck, coming in at thirteen to one, followed by Spitkid, King Neptune, Heap O'Rhythm, and Izanami.

And Izanami. And this one hurts. It hurts like a hammer on his rib cage, like a lit match against his ear. Emma-O looked at him, his posture slipping, slumping forward. "Are you having a heart attack?" she asked, half-seriously.

Connor talked without turning his head. "When I was a kid we used to stand by the rail. Let's go down there for the last race."

"Just don't have a heart attack," Emma-O smiled, squeezing his hand.

The world flattened out at the bottom, opened up before him as Connor leaned against the rail, breathed through his nose, tried to take it in. He let his racing form drop to the ground.

Emma-O smoked a cigarette and studied him. "Have you like, lost a lot of money today or something?"

"Don't be smart," Connor said. Lips thick. The bugle sounded. "We'll go right after this one."

The announcer went through his routine as the horses sauntered out for the last race. Connor ignored the jockeys, watching the horses carefully, their muscled movements, twitching tails and bobbing heads. The number-eight horse, a grey called Free Rein, lagged in line. A beautiful mottled grey, but all Connor could see was the rich black of its eyes as it passed him by.

"I like Macy's Rainbow," Emma-O said.

"Take this," Connor said, pressing the roll of bills into her hand, "and go bet number eight. Two thousand on number eight. Free Rein."

"That's a silly name. And, mister odds, it's a long shot on the board. Take a look."

Connor put his head down on the rail. "Please just go bet it."

"Okaay, grumpy guts," she sang, walking away.

The last race was a mile long. At six furlongs Free Rein had moved all the way to the inside rail and was running away with it as they thundered past. Connor looked at the odds board, did a quick calculation, and considered the unbreathable prospect of winning forty thousand dollars, his lungs filled to the brim with burning paper money. When his focus caught the race again, it was just in time to see Free Rein die, the rest of the pack surging ahead of him. In a photo-finish it was Macy's Rainbow, Raja-Yama, and Couldyawin.

Emma-O came bounding up. "I missed it, who won?"

Connor put his head back down on the rail. There was some kind of worm writhing in his belly, some kind of beetle burrowing into his heart. "Macy's fucking Rainbow," he spit.

Emma-O moved up behind him. "Good, because that's the horse I bet," she said in his ear.

Connor twisted his head around to look at her, hearing the rubbing of little stones at the base of his skull.

Emma-O tucked the ticket into his shirt pocket and pointed to the oversized digital numbers. "And, thanks to me, you just won over seven thousand dollars."

"Excellent," Connor breathed, taking out the ticket. And kissed her.

Expecting thank you, Emma-O cocked her head. "I'm sorry, what did you say, Connor-Cruise?"

"I said excellent. The situation is excellent. My centre gives way, my right is in retreat; situation excellent. I shall attack."

Emma-O stepped back, waving off like a referee. Laughing. "Okay, now I don't know what you're talking about."

"Marshall Foch, first battle of the Marne, World War One."

"Uh-huh," said Emma-O, bobbing her head. "Well, now that we've had our fun, and history lessons too, can we go? Your friends will be waiting for you."

Connor turned, smiled. Grabbed her hand. "You're right, they will be. You go ahead and hold them. I'm just going to go cash this and then see a man about a horse. I'll be right out."

"Man about a horse ... okaay Connor-Cruise," she said with a kiss, then spun and walked away.

Connor watched Emma-O go through the turnstiles, watched her waggle her way out to the parking lot, obscured and then lost behind the streams of people funnelled to the exits as the place poured itself out. For a few minutes he stood there, still, letting the air reach into his collar. Closing his eyes, listening, that unmistakable whirring over his head. Then, in one movement, fluid, a pivot and arc, he jumped over the rail, landed on the dirt of the racetrack, and started running.

dead motorcycle cops

As long as Steven and Walter stayed together, they would be okay; Oscher could not get them. It was a simple, almost scientific verdict, mutually concluded after many discussions, trials, even bruising errors in the controlled environment of their little town (maybe a hundred people at most, now that the grain elevator was shut down). It was a small-knowledge world, where facts were few but hard and proven. One had to swallow them whole. Steven and Walter knew the town limits like the thinness of their own skin, knew they were all each other had. They needed each other, were bound to each other by all sorts of contracts in blood and spit and the express language of ten-year-old boys. *After all, we're best friends*, Steven said. That was something to believe in.

On the day of the disappearances they were playing Dead Motorcycle Cops. They chased each other all over town, heaving into their bike pedals to get momentum, get some speed going before tucking their feet up, crouching down low, streamlined, sweat burning their eyes as they peered through the cages of their hockey helmets, keeping a bead on each other, imagining sirens, the steel glaze of pursuit. But always keeping a look out for Oscher.

On the long gravel road that ran beside the fairgrounds, Walter slowed down. Standing on his pedals, his body stretched forward over the handlebars, he stared hard at something by the side of the road. Wobbling, he pulled up to it, slid down on his bike. He took his helmet off. Steven came up beside him, braking fast, crunching gravel. "Holy shit," he said, nostrils flaring in the afternoon heat.

A cat, long and grey like lead, lay destroyed in the grass, its eyes squeezed tight, legs twisted and splayed. Twine trailed from where it had been tied around its neck. Red and blue muck oozed from its mouth. Beside it were two dead sparrows, broken things arranged like lovers to face each other. Flies buzzed, squirming over the cat's teeth. Steven looked up and down the road, scanned the empty fairgrounds, peered back at the railway tracks. Listening. Oscher would be around, somewhere. There wasn't a sound. The sky hurt Steven's eyes with blue, the blazing blue of late summer that irradiated the mind, made him feel the piling clouds above him, their lambent bellies burnt, bruised. A big black bird perched on a fence pole, twitching, watching them with liquid eyes from across the ditch. Its wing glistened with the sheen of cobalt.

Walter felt something rising, the taste of sick at the back of his throat.

"I gotta go to the can," he said, his voice trailing.

"So go," Steven shrugged. "Just go in the ditch. I'll stand guard."

Walter slouched, dipped his head. A long gob of spit wound down from his parted lips. "I gotta do the other thing. I gotta sit down."

Steven groaned. "All right, let's go to the Legion."

The shadow of the Legion Hall loomed over the corner of the fairgrounds. It wasn't used much anymore, ever since they built the community centre on the other side of town, and Walter didn't like going in there, thought the building looked used and sore, the weeds and peeling paint and smell of things done a long time ago always made him think of graveyards, of being somewhere he didn't need to be. But Steven was already taking his bike from him, hiding it with his under the front steps. He took a quick look over his shoulder before lifting out the basement window.

It was always so dark inside, before their eyes could adjust. But the grey cement walls felt nice, cool against Walter's hands as he dropped down to the floor.

"Okay, so go," Steven said, giving him a little push towards the bathroom. Then he went around the corner to the kitchen. Walter thought about Steven sitting on the counter there, drinking a glass of water, waiting patiently for him, like he owned the place, and that image made Walter feel something, he wasn't sure, he couldn't quite tell, it almost seemed like sadness, like a craving, he wanted to say something but there was really no way, because he also felt ashamed.

The light in the bathroom was sickly yellow, made Walter look alien in the black-speckled mirror. Inside the stall it smelled like old, still water. So quiet in there. He didn't feel retchy anymore and he certainly didn't have to crap but he had to do something or Steven would get mad.

Walter took his glasses off, put them on the floor, stared blankly at the belt around his ankles, how out of focus it looked like a snake. *There were so many things that could kill you*, he thought. Sometimes he would hold his head under the bathwater and go as still as he could, pretending like a dream, *This is what it must be like*. He didn't want to think about death all the time; it just seemed to come to him. Really, he never wanted to kill anything. He wasn't like that, wasn't insane or rabid like Julian Oscher. Walter's mom didn't like to hear that. "Now listen, Walt," she started, sitting him down at the kitchen table. This after the time he and Steven had caught Oscher laying dead gophers on the railway tracks, when he had looked up and saw them there in the weeds by the embankment, and started throwing the mutilated little corpses at them in great, blood-flicking arcs. Walt ran home screaming that day, bits of guts stuck to his face and neck, screaming that *Julian Oscher was crazy*, Walter's mom had to calm him down, put her hand on his arm, hold him there. "Not everyone is like you, Walter. Some people are different. That's what Julian is. That's why he goes to a special school in the city. He's just ... different."

It made Walter tired to think of all this. He closed his eyes. He heard a thump from the kitchen, then a plastic glass rattling across the floor. Rolling away. "Hey Steve!" he called. "Whaddya doing?" His voice rang, echoed around. "Steve?"

Suddenly Walter could sense that someone was in the bathroom with him. He scrunched down to see under the stall door, saw the blur of bare feet. Quickly he reached for his glasses but a hand snatched them away. It scared him, and the tears were making it even harder to see.

"Steve, quit screwing around! I mean it!"

Walter listened hard, could hear nothing but a boiling in his ears.

"Steve!"

Someone exhaling through their nose.

"Steeeeeeeve!"

He couldn't breathe. He knew he was going to pass out soon. None of this was his fault.

"Steve?"

early rounds

Victory's early fortunes rise and fall with her parents. Her mother is constant, smiling close up, an abstraction of buoyancy and light. Her father Earl is removed, elusive, gravity-seeking at the corner of things, somehow more important. He is a semisuccessful boxer – semisuccessful because he likes to drink, actually he loves it. Dreams for it. When he can't drink, when he is training and suffering and the dreaming is deepest, he goes around slamming doors.

After a doomed title shot (the champion, a Korean, cunningly uses his face to break Earl's right hand), he retires, buys a house along the coast. At the top of a hill, overlooking the ocean, it is perfect in its height and whiteness and opacity all around. Victory loves it there, *location location location* she hears on the television one day, it makes such perfect sense, everyone wants to be near water. Swimming makes Victory ache, ache inside to swim all the time, later in memory she is a little girl swimming in rapture, immersed in the fluid magic of sparkling vastness that God calls the ocean.

The ocean is my motion – she hears that somewhere too, sings it to herself in beamy loops. Victory is a good swimmer, sleek and efficient; as she moves her mouth drinks air like it's the future. When her stomach hurts (only sometimes) she turns over on her back, straightens out thin and divine, packs her eyes with cloud. Victory owns her own movements, feels the force of her will as significant. In the water, she can go anywhere she wants to. Her little sister Pyrrhic stays on the beach, sits with her pad of acid-free paper and paints the same picture over and over again, blue on blue with whirls of white, airy and pretty. Reading one of her books about sticks and coins, their mother says that Fate has given each of them a special talent.

cut

Victory's stomach starts to hurt more and more. Pain comes at her in rushes. A doctor pushes between folds of her skin with two fingers, watches her wince, talks to her mother. Victory goes into the hospital to have her appendix removed. *That was a big one*, the doctor tells Victory afterwards. *Very inflamed.*

Victory's family visits. Pyrrhic brings her paintings, new ones with touches of fire, red in a swirling sky, the paper curled at the edges. Visiting hours are over at eight o'clock. On the drive home one night her dad is mesmerized by a passing car, by the sight of two little Asian girls crowding their heads out the window, laughing into the open air. He swerves into them. Both cars careen off the road, jumping like angry beetles.

judges

The funeral is poorly attended. Some mob types are there, smelling like cigarettes. They have money and damp hands.

corner

Victory goes to live with her aunt in Saskatoon, Saskatchewan. It is a small city in the middle of a flat, dry place. It is a city full of practical, modest people who make common leaps of false logic. Victory loathes them. She tries tarot cards, extended bouts of staring and willing. But the ocean remains long gone.

Her aunt is severely single. She has a wide array of rules and expectations of the detailed, insignificant sort, the ordered life with no plan. She teaches Victory how to clean things properly (*properly!*) but dust is a persistent enemy. With puberty Victory puts on weight, grows sullen. Her only friend Roxanne sees this, asks indulgently how it is to live there. *It makes me hungry*, Victory replies. Victory skips her high school graduation to move into a tiny corner suite at the top of a four-storey building downtown. There are no skyscrapers in a city like this.

trainers

Victory and Roxanne get jobs at the same office. They process data. They are at the bottom of the white-collar world where everyone wears clean clothes. *You girls run this place, you know*, their supervisor says, staring at their tits.

stick and move

Victory watches the news. Standing before bodies of Islamic insurgents, a government official in Tajikistan explains, through a sheen of sweat and slipping smiles, that violence just happens, *violence just happens in a dynamic society*. Victory likes the roominess of the answer. Any explanation is appreciated. It's better than nothing, better than just sitting there stuffing handfuls of Cheerios into her mouth. When a Russian submarine lies powerless at the bottom of the Bering Sea, Victory dreams of a giant fish with metal skin gently dying in mid-swim.

DARRYL JOEL BERGER

weigh-in

Victory and Roxanne try a new diet: fat-burning soup. Three cups of V8 juice, one carrot, three or four green onions, one can of tomatoes, one-half head of cabbage, one can of green beans, one green pepper, five stalks of celery, one package of soup mix, one cube of bouillon, two cups of water. Chop up the vegetables. Add everything into a pot. Mix. Boil quickly. After ten minutes, turn down the heat to simmer, keep stirring until all the vegetables are tender.

There is a seven-day regimen that follows, the only constant being the consumption of soup. On Day One you also get to eat fruit – cantaloupe and watermelon being lowest in calories and therefore best. At the end of Day Two is the reward of a baked potato (with butter). Day Three is more fruit. Day Four, hump day, brings bananas and skim milk. For Day Five you can choose between ten to twenty ounces of beef or up to six fresh tomatoes. Day Six is beef and vegetables day, all you want. And on Day Seven you get brown rice, unsweetened fruit juice, and more vegetables. *Congratulations*, the recipe reads, *you just lost ten to fifteen pounds*.

Yet Victory's recipe reads somewhat differently. Day One and Two run well enough, promises and appeals and afternoon stomach-kneading seeing her through. She can imagine melting away. But Day Three is sick with the simmering affliction of soup, the taste of it, its blandness and vile texture. A salad comes as recompense, still healthy, but then the Italian dressing. The full implosion always arrives on Day Four, fast-food never tasting so good, so damned good, while the soup sits despised in the fridge, a false prophet. There is never a Day Five.

body blow

Victory squints to see it, screwing her face up disdainfully. The sun sits pulsing in the sky against her, perfect and triumphant in its clean sheet of cloudless blue. This, after she prayed so hard for rain. Just one little storm, she had prayed, staring down at The Tower.

The company barbecue is fifty or so people navigating the front lawn of the office building with paper plates and inappropriate shoes. Gathering in clusters. Roxanne is not among them, having phoned in sick to go shopping for clothes, having lost thirty pounds from the fat-burning soup, boundless energy and interest in everything now, posture and hair products and especially clothes, their colours and combinations.

Victory stands off to the side, alone, not even tasting her third hamburger, a blocky shape against the heat, her insides boiling against her, seething at herself, at every one of her two hundred and thirty-three pounds, desperately hating everyone.

jab

Victory comes home to messages that are not for her, someone's elderly mother pleading *Please call, we haven't heard from you in such a long time.* The messages themselves don't bother Victory so much as the disappointed, disembodied muttering at the end when the old woman hands the phone back to her husband to hang up on the wall.

clinch

A rocket named Mariana explodes on the launch pad in the jungles of French Guyana. A nine-year-old Scottish girl who is allergic to water has her specially designed raincoat stolen in a home burglary. After a televised appeal from her parents, the coat is anonymously returned but the thieves have shredded it. Flooding and mudslides in Venezuela kill tens of thousands. A massive cyclone wrecks Bangladesh. Iran is devastated by an earthquake. There is vicious sectarian violence, widespread rioting and looting in Belfast. A giant tsunami obliterates East Java and Bali. Victory watches it all, fills herself with it. The televised noise of the world sounds like a death-rattle to her ears, and she cheers it.

combinations

Suddenly the weather is surprising, confusing. Inspiring fear. Then it simply stops. All over the globe, all at once, the sky crowds with cloud. Day after day, bit by bit, it fills itself in. Scientists sputter or shake their heads, although one blames teflon. Everything becomes darker and darker.

People are inspired in their bad behaviour. The Shining Path assassinates seven judges in one day. An American congressman murders an intern, then his family, then himself. The Japanese Red Army blows up a NATO conference. India invades Pakistan, then China invades India. The Russian government is angry and menacing, feels left out but consoles itself with exterminating the Chechens. When a teller in Detroit doesn't move fast enough, a robber shoots her and all fourteen other people in the bank. Two nihilistic, love-struck German teenagers kill their parents, a neighbour, a school teacher, a policeman, a postman, and a dog. A man in full Klingon uniform starts shooting at a Star Trek convention in Mesquite, Texas, killing eleven before a burly Captain Kirk brains him with a phaser. Ethicists call it *mass expressions of degeneracy*. Victory stops going to work, eats and sleeps in front of her television.

The sky, literally, is falling. Every morning is dimmer. The ceiling of cloud looms lower. It makes you stand and stare. Blankness. People say things like *doomsday* and *end of the world*. They go crazy. The news, while it lasts, is appalling, thrilling. *This is zero-hour for mankind*, the announcer says.

late rounds

The electricity goes out. Then the water.

decision

The sirens have finally stopped. Victory stands on the edge of the roof in her swimsuit, arms out, balancing, her feet halfway into the air. There is nothing to see now, the whole world choked by rolling cloud, all around. You can reach out and touch it. The air is heavy and almost silent, only the distant sound of rushing water, you can barely hear it, somewhere close but beyond. One by one Victory tosses recipe cards into the nothingness. Then she assumes a diver's pose.

not invited to
    the photographs

The photograph (colour, 4 x 6, matte finish) is slightly tilted, just enough to get all of me in. I'm wearing a tuxedo, standing in the front yard of the house I grew up in, grinning behind a cigarette. My nephew is off to the side, half out of frame. He's wearing a diaper and nothing else except those locks of blonde hair that only babies have. He's looking up at the camera like it's a hovering spacecraft. My mom is the picture-taker. She's babysitting for my brother that weekend, and I'm seven minutes away (a cigarette is seven minutes long, according to survival manuals) from driving into Saskatoon for a wedding. The yard looks really green, it always does in these pictures, much greener than I ever remember it.

I'm an usher for my friend Bethany's wedding. I'll be late. It hardly matters; she has four ushers, which is at least two too many, even for a wedding this size. The most I'll do is say hello to some people from school (who are slightly too eager to know what I'm doing these days) and take some pictures of the bride as she comes up the sidewalk. It's windy, and her dress wants to whip like a long white flag.

At a certain point in the ceremony the four bridesmaids will turn away from the guests and face the altar. I think to myself: *those dresses do not flatter their wide backs.* And then: *we're all getting older.*

After the wedding two of the other ushers will have a conversation in which Warren asks Dalton where the pictures are being taken, and Dalton tells Warren not to worry about it. Warren is sure that Bethany wants us in the pictures. Dalton is sure that we are not invited. Warren is wearing a look of polite confusion on his face while I just stand there waiting for inertia to take over. Warren is one of Bethany's special-episode friends (in this case, the year she spent in Montreal) and his knowledge is only snapshot-deep. Dalton is the groom's older brother and *his* knowledge has the weight of his big meaty head; he knows that I've slept with the bride and three of the four bridesmaids (Lauren, Lisa, Bailey but not Karrie and no, don't be ridiculous, not all at once, it takes years). Dalton reminds me of JR from the television show *Dallas*. When he walks away, he has that same flushed look that Larry Hagman always had.

I will never be Warren's friend but for the next two hours we are bound like brothers. We walk the two blocks to the hotel where the reception will be. It is the best hotel in the city, with a facade like a castle. The Queen has slept here. I've only been inside once before, when I took my mom for brunch and a fancy cup of tea.

Warren and I will sit in the dark-wood bar and drink imported beer, waiting until it's time to go up to the reception. Warren is still confused about being excluded from the pictures. I change the topic. We talk about being single and he is duly worried about not having found someone. I tell him that if it hasn't happened yet, it's probably not going to.

At the reception Warren and I will be seated at the "singles" table. There's a lawyer from Regina with skin like ground chalk but also long, curly black hair and white stockings. She's like an upscale gypsy, these blue half-moons high on her cheekbones. I try to talk to her but she's the eyes-diverted type.

The master of ceremonies is an old guy (some uncle or honorary uncle) with enormous black glasses, the kind I've only seen in magazines like *Vanity Fair*, and there only on the faces of Hollywood moguls. He reads jokes out a copy of

Reader's Digest, holding out the magazine at arm's length. People try to laugh but the silverware is louder. *Huh? Huh?* the old guy goes.

There will be a point during dinner where I look up to see that my twenty-something server has been replaced by a middle-aged black woman whose nametag identifies her as WILLA, a SUPERVISOR from LAUNDRY SERVICES, and instead of a server's black and white uniform she's wearing a big green smock with chemical-coloured stains on her belly and breasts. She pours me coffee and smiles. Soon the news will emerge that the hotel staff has gone on strike. I look up at the head table to see Bethany flushed and vibrating but I cannot deny that the Cajun Crusted Salmon Filet (served with citrus fennel sauce) was excellent.

There are the usual toasts and speeches. The reception room is cavernous and I can't always hear. Then Bailey goes up and starts singing along to a karaoke machine, while her boyfriend accompanies on guitar. One verse in and she starts crying. By the middle of the second verse she is no longer singing at all, just sobbing into the microphone, moaning along to the lyrics. The boyfriend is bug-eyed, helpless. Lauren and Lisa come and take her away. When the boyfriend can't figure out how to turn off the karaoke machine, and the music just keeps going on and on, Warren will go up and unplug it.

The groomsmen are like spiky little sportscars. They have names like Carlo or Woody or Monty or something. They will keep coming up to me and asking me how I'm doing, showing me their teeth. I smoke, look up, look down, say I'm fine. Everything seems lit through. There is a giant circle of Celtic pattern working its way around the ceiling. The carpets are that dark red like blood, reminding me of a shirt I had once that said ALABAMA CRIMSON TIDE. After repeated trips to the open bar (half manned by two drunken cousins) I discover they have some very expensive Scotch.

The band will cancel the day before, so instead there is only a disc jockey. He has a blazer with sparkles on it. By request or some kind of *Muriel's Wedding* fixation he plays a lot of ABBA, and it's the usual thing where the dance floor is filled with old people and children. Anyone twenty-five to thirty-five goes upstairs to party in the rooms. I only come back down for drinks.

On one trip Bethany will surprise me, grab me by the arm. *Where were you guys for the pictures?* she asks. It's strange to see her up close in that dress. Even as she's trying to talk to me some uncle is leading her away for a dance.

Save one for me! I call, heading for the elevator.

A few hours later I'll be lying on a king-size bed while a party winds down around me. I prop my head up with pillows, rest a beer can on my chest. Karrie is reclining beside me. Neither Warren or the girl with the curly black hair are anywhere in my field of vision. Karrie whispers in my ear: *Wouldn't it be great if all these people just left?*

Yes, I will say, *that would indeed be great.* I'm tired, like I'm always tired when I drink other people's liquor.

Bailey will help Karrie shoo everyone from the room. *Come on everybody, let's go, I'm beat*, Karrie says. It gets quiet and darker, one of those gloomy hotel lamps on a desk in the corner. I listen to the fan from the bathroom. I fall asleep.

When I wake up Karrie will be kneeling over me, her white, wet breasts falling out of her bathrobe. *You're wearing too many clothes*, she will say, pulling my belt like a rip chord.

In the morning the hotel room will seem pushed in, in fact the curtains are too hot to look at. Something smells sour. Karrie says I need to get up and get going. Patting myself down I discover that a roll of film is missing from my jacket. Karrie says she'll look for it later.

I'll drive home in my tuxedo. My mom will ask me if I'm going back for the gift opening. *No*, I'll say, *I got all the pictures I need*, knowing that I'll never see any of them ever again.

the prince
(sometimes you're dying)

How Many Kinds Of Principalities There Are, And By What Means They Are Acquired

It is 1978 sunshine. The Lawyer makes a hypnotist's face at the abridged biography of William the Conqueror he holds in his right hand. His left hand holds out a coffee mug. Tammy Dixon stands above him, bends forward at the waist, pours the Lawyer coffee, quietly informs him that she is carrying his child. Ten months out of community college (Office Administration and Management) she is calm, decided, wears a creamy pant-suit with copper-ringed buttons.

Concerning New Principalities Which Are Acquired By One's Own Arms And Ability

The Lawyer wails. Gobbing tears flow relentlessly, hopelessly; in blotted ruin he tries to hide his head from this sudden comet of disaster streaking across his sky. Tammy stands there. Holding the pot of coffee. It's as light as anything. The weight from her whole body settles on her hips. She understands what she's doing: determination is key because the future can be money.

Concerning New Principalities Which Are Acquired Either By The Arms Of Others Or By Good Fortune

And then quickly the Lawyer promises everything, apologizes for everything else. The Lawyer says he's *sorry so sorry* but really he's only sorry for himself. His instincts tell him to negotiate. After the right amount of resistance Tammy Dixon agrees that, yes, discretion is the main thing. And security.

Concerning Those Who Have Obtained A Principality By Wickedness

In actual fact, conception occurs on a kitchen counter, Tammy's uncle Dean hooking her legs with his elbows, pushing them higher and higher until she looks like a wishbone.

Concerning The Way In Which The Strength Of All Principalities Ought To Be Measured

It's twins. Tammy wants to be a good mom, thinks in terms of improvement and a better life, nothing specific. Being happy herself seems a good first step. She joins a gym, starts bowling again, goes out dancing on Ladies' Night. Her own mom babysits, doesn't mind at all. Two nights a week Tammy hauls Dave and Dino to a class called Water Babies but after a while it's just too much. The boys can learn to swim when they're older.

Concerning The Secretaries Of Princes

Maternity-leave ends. Tammy does not go back to work. The Lawyer continues to issue her a paycheque. Otherwise he is not involved. After one of their conversations Tammy has to look in a dictionary for the phrase *status quo.*

Concerning Mixed Principalities

The twins at two are not exactly hell but most of the time Tammy still feels like both guard and prisoner. The house is full of ashtrays and half-smoked cigarettes. She craves escape.

Everyone grows into their roles. Dino is a quiet child, prefers to play alone, watches shows about cyborg dinosaurs and monkeys who travel through time. Dave has dynamite in him, jumps down stairs two at a time, forces Dino up trees, drags him into cardboard theatres where they re-enact war movies. Their great uncle brings toys that go largely ignored.

That Which Concerns A Prince On The Subject Of The Art Of War

In *Defeated* there are only two things to be. A third thing exists – *Surrender Guy* – but you don't take that one if you're normal. Because Surrender Guys get tied-up and blindfolded and kicked in the ass. Or pushed into the ditch by the woods, maybe even pissed on. Only Myron Anderson up the lane wants to be a Surrender Guy. And he's retarded. So really there's only two things to be.

"And what's that?" Tammy asks, thinking about the dirt-track races, new shoes, hands on her breasts, highlights for her hair, anything.

'Well," Dave starts, "sometimes you're dead ..."

"And sometimes you're dying," Dino finishes. To illustrate, he throws himself into convulsions on the floor. Dave dances around like a boxing champion.

Concerning Hereditary Principalities

School is compromised. Always there is: *yes, but.* Dino is a good student but too withdrawn. Dave has personality bursting but he cannot sit still, charges around after other kids on the playground, tries to clothesline them. Tammy finds elementary schoolteachers arrogant. They look at her and presume things. They don't know her boys at all, have no idea what's in them. "As long as they're both passing," Tammy says, getting up to leave.

Concerning A Civil Principality

Dino and Dave can look after themselves. The house is like a tomb. Tammy trolls the town for men and vodka Paralyzers. Dino stays in his room, reads Japanese comic books and plays computer games. Muscle-bound monsters wearing

German helmets breathe fire through his dreams. Dave goes out with his buddies, takes martial arts, does part-time jobs and circles cars in the classifieds. Sometimes he throws bottles at people. It's no big thing.

That One Should Avoid Being Despised And Hated
Tammy is waving the bayonet as she talks, as she lectures about how a fifteen-year-old shouldn't have a bayonet hidden in his room, shouldn't have a bayonet to begin with: "... under your pillow, for Christ's sake!"
Dave hardly listens. What the fuck, he's going to start taking lectures from old whore-bags?

Concerning Cruelty And Clemency, And Whether It Is Better To Be Loved Than Feared
Tammy can't be an angry-guts with Dino for very long. Guilt squeezes her stomach, twists its fingers in her, forces her into his room at night. He's such a beautiful child, tall and thin, big blue eyes, good skin, eyelashes that make you murmur.

How A Prince Should Conduct Himself As To Gain Renown
Graduation. Tammy Dixon is proud, proud, proud. Who wouldn't be? Not one but two fine boys up there, her handsome princes. Afterwards they mug for the camera, give Tammy the finger.

How Many Kinds Of Soldiery There Are, And Concerning Mercenaries
Dave joins the Army. His test scores are average but the recruiter is desperate: foreign theatres demand fresh bodies. Dave thinks airborne will totally kick ass.

Concerning The Way In Which Princes Should Keep Faith
Dino climbs out a window in the middle of the night. The stars spin and slide, inspire inside grins and maybe philosophy. It's difficult to know what to do in life. He feels his ideas

more than he understands them. Sometimes he can move in that answer's direction. There's a pulse to guide him. But lately Dino feels nothing. Now the problem becomes academic, something to solve, something needing a plan. "You'll never be happy without a plan," Tammy tells him, reciting words from a doctor on the radio. "Everyone wants to be happy." But Dino just wants to get high.

Dino likes to get high on freon because it is (a) free and (b) accessible: every car, home, trailer has some, you just need a pair of pliers and a drinking straw (a pen with its guts pulled out will do, in a pinch). Quality can be a problem – usually the freon's been in the unit for a couple of years, absorbing oil from the compressor, chemicals from the welds in the lines, all sorts of shit. Pure freon is tasteless, odourless, but dirty freon tastes like sugar. Also, too much freon can burn your lungs out or make your heart stop.

How Flatterers Should Be Avoided

His friend Damien calls it huffing. "It's just molecules, man," he says. "Suck 'em in." School is a land of vicious reptiles but Damien's cool, is there to catch Dino the first time he blacks out. Since then Dino's learned to position himself to fall down straight, like a collapsing jack-in-the-box. Since then Dino spends almost every night huffing on any air conditioner that isn't in plain sight of the street. The why is irrelevant.

The last time Dino got high with Damien: the look of floating joy on Damien's face as he dipped in tight circles with his arms out, "Hey, I'm a plane! A plane, boss! A plane!" Then he tripped on his own stutter-step, crash-landed on his face. The doctor at Emergency said he was lucky not to lose his tongue.

Concerning Things For Which Men, And Especially Princes, Are Praised Or Blamed

It is the middle of the night. Dave's arm is broken. His chest feels dense, squished. Mouth full of blood. He is kneeling in the soft dirt of a ploughed field, his hands tied behind his back. An excited man with a flashlight and an old rifle barks at Dave in a language that he doesn't understand, will never understand. It's all lies anyway.

Half a mile away a house is on fire, trees in the yard lurid and ghastly. The air all around is the richest blue-black. It rings with the sound of the man's voice as he circles, as he yells and makes dust. He is ranting, working himself up. Dave closes his eyes. Sways a little. On the inside he is dreaming. There's no sense listening.

The Princes Have Lost Their States

Dino is huffing and huffing. His heart is beating faster and faster. His ears close, go *pop pop pop*. The street light from the corner whirls into his head. Maybe it's God. He's so full and happy, feels his grin all the way through his nervous system, follows it all the way along like wires, tingling his toes. He closes his eyes, *wham* and down, the elevatoring falls, *whewwwww*. Whew. He hopes he doesn't vomit.

What Fortune Can Effect In Human Affairs, And How To Withstand Her

There is a channel – one of those higher, useless channels that no one ever goes to – that shows, late at night, a still picture of the earth from space. He's watched it for hours, sometimes until morning, transfixed. The feeling one gets is one of being infinitely removed. Above. It's a nice thing to think about, in the end.

the indisputable weight
of the ocean

It was a simple enough thing and that thing was simply this: Edmund Kelley was a gentleman. Of course his mom called him her *little gentleman*, as in "Oh Edmund, you are my perfect little gentleman," which did seem to hold to a certain logic that these type of things often follow, considering her affection for him and the fact that he was, after all, only ten years old. Still, Edmund himself was not particularly fond of the diminutive aspect of that title. Gentleman was enough; gentleman summed up the whole thing rather nicely, thank you.

He was definitely a more refined version of your average child. He lived in a state of perpetual Sunday mornings. He stood before you with such composure: his shiny blonde hair combed into a nice, neat part, his clothes as clean as they had been in the closet, without rumples or rips or tears or stains. And in his manner he was like a little man trying to impress someone's parents, listening when spoken to, smiling politely, saying "Please." Indeed, adults liked Edmund very much, and that suited him just fine.

They lived on an acreage at the edge of a small town by the sea. "An estate," his mom said. For as long as Edmund could remember, it had been just the two of them, his dad working far away in classified locations. This was to be expected; he was, after all, a nuclear submarine commander.

Edmund did not go to school. "You're such a smart one," his mother said. "It's best if I just teach you at home."

"I concur completely," Edmund agreed. It only made sense; his mom was a wonderful teacher and, since he had no others, they were the best of friends.

Edmund did not have much use for other children. The only time he saw any was when they went into town for groceries, and what he saw he did not like. From the back seat of the car he might spy some running amuck in the park or dawdling aimlessly in front of the store. They seemed hopeless and wild all at once. "That bunch lacks any semblance of discipline," Edmund would say to his mom.

"Oh honey, they're just grubby little kids, nothing to worry about," his mom replied. "They won't bite." But to Edmund they looked like they just might do exactly that.

If such a thing can actually be enjoyed then Edmund enjoyed order. Peace and quiet and order. He prided himself on the neatness of his room, on the orderly way he kept his things. And while he had many things, from trains to model planes to amateur scientist sets, what Edmund loved the most, what he lined his walls with like the bricks of Tutankahman's tomb, were his books. The most prized were from his dad, sent in parcels of brown paper that, if smelled hard enough, had the faint and mysterious scent of what could only be the deep sea.

The summer of Edmund's eleventh birthday revealed itself to be a most tumultuous time. For some vague reasons of economics that his mom refused to give Edmund a chance to understand, they had to move to the city. It was all very upsetting. Edmund said, "This is terrible."

"Oh honey please, it's only the suburbs," his mom said.

Terrible, Edmund thought.

And it was. Suddenly there were people everywhere, all around them, all the time. They were surrounded by people. Deluged by people. The houses on either side seemed to bob in the shadows a mere few arm's-lengths apart. Cars and dogs and babies in carriages and old men who muttered in what Edmund could only assume was profane language, and children, especially *children* seethed all around their new home. *These people will sink us*, Edmund thought with a shudder.

Edmund wondered out loud if Dad might be able to take leave and come see them in their new house.

"He's on a very important mission right now," his mom said.

It must be dangerous too, Edmund thought, *to make Mom look so distracted and tired.*

But Edmund was not without consideration for his mom. And because he did not want to be an extra burden on her, he tried to cope with his new situation. He really did. He taped a picture of Winston Churchill to his mirror to remind himself not to complain. In fact he tried to be as inconspicuous as possible, to stay out of his mom's way and let her get herself grounded. So when she announced that she would now be out of the house during the day, that she would be starting a job, he gave himself a headache with the energy it took not to say anything about how absolutely terrible that was. "You're a big boy now and it's only for a few hours a day," his mom said.

And Edmund thought, *Et tu, Bruté?*

Then the noises came.

It was the second afternoon by himself and he was in his favourite chair by the window in his bedroom, reading a fascinating deconstruction of Napoleon's last campaign at Waterloo (*Not so much the fault of the great man as his incompetent subordinates*, Edmund thought) when he heard the most horrifying screams next door. His blood froze. The screaming continued. Someone was begging, pleading for mercy. A boy's voice. Should he call the police? But then, what was *that*? Laughter? It was. Big, pealing, squealing laughter. And now what, more screams? Edmund went to the window to investigate but the houses were too close together – he could see nothing. He was fairly certain that the commotion was coming from the neighbour's backyard, but once outside he was again thwarted, this time by the height of the fence and the closeness of its slats. *It's like the bloody Berlin wall,* Edmund thought. Still, he could hear them on the other side.

It sounded like there were two of them and one was torturing the other. Having quite a good time of it too, laughing hysterically the whole while. Some kind of foreign instrument was involved, possibly a hose. The victim would periodically make an attempt to wrest away control of this object, there was a good deal of running and physical grappling, and often there were violent sprays of water in the air. All Edmund could think about was the Roman coliseum and the blood sport of gladiators. He went into the house to lie down.

His mom found him on the living room couch with a damp towel over his face. "What's wrong, dear? Are you sick?"

"Just relaxing, mom. I'm fine." He did not want to worry her.

Besides, it might never happen again.

Which of course was foolish optimism. The next afternoon they were at it with a vengeance, this time with some sort of inflated ball that they delighted in throwing at each other as hard as they could, undoubtedly with the intent of causing maximum injury because there was some rather plaintive sobbing, much different than the hysterics of the day before, and some angry yelling from an adult within the house. Then the injured party laughed at the one who was scolded and the whole thing began again. *Sadists!* Edmund thought.

Sleep offered no escape for Edmund. His head swam with images of fire and barbaric pagan rituals, of silhouetted figures with demonically painted faces. It was sheer, unadulterated terror.

The next day, tired and bleary eyed, he found himself crouched in the shade of the fence again, listening to more carnage. Today the violence was more straightforward, revolving around some kind of whacking. They whacked and teased and cursed and whooped and tormented and ... what was that? They were keeping score! *They were actually keeping score.* That was too much. Even the sun seemed to blaze with indignation.

When he entered the alley Edmund had no idea what he was going to do. He still had no idea when he silently, breathlessly pushed open the gate to the demons' yard.

There were two of them. One was bigger, older and he had an oversized plastic bat. The other one was more Edmund's size, although thicker. He had the inflated ball. They were playing ... *what, some kind of baseball?* It looked nothing like the version Edmund had seen in the *Encyclopedia Brittanica*. There was only home plate and first base, signified by a frisbee and a dirty rag respectively. The hitter had to get to first base and back without getting tagged. The pitcher had to retrieve the hit ball and then tag – nail, really – the runner, the more force the better, so it seemed. They called each other the cruelest of names. It was all ... madness. Edmund stood there and watched, transfixed. After some time the smaller one, the pitcher, squinted into the sun and saw him there in the corner. "Hey!" he called out. "Whaddya doing there?"

His voice rang like doom in Edmund's ears. In the next few swirling moments his mind went completely and utterly blank. "My dad's a nuclear submarine commander," he heard himself say.

"No shit?" said the older one.

"Hey," said the pitcher. "Hey, I'm getting killed here. You wanna play outfield?"

And because his mind was still a frothing emptiness, because he could think of nothing else to say, he simply nodded.

God he had fun that day.

All the wives were burned alive. All the wives but one. Four out of five. Too many and not enough. Then the other thoughts took over.

The scientists – the husbands, the men, the prisoners, the disgraced – were out on the lake. They wanted to go fishing. Take the boat out. It was always something – fishing, hiking, picnics, bullshit – to make something out of the day. They were like little boys that way, always this thing with the group. Looking for escape where there was none, at me their sad warden in a place with no walls. Me, the No-No Man. Among them but not them. Worse but better. Of course they were too polite not to invite me; after all the boat held six.

We were all surprised by the meteor shower. The scientists loved it, oblivious to the danger, how we made such a nice, tight target for God's hot stones. For them it was just colour, something to chat about later, *the radiant point is an issue of perspective, la-di-da-di-da,* always this thing where they talked around the circumstances they found themselves in. Non-persons non-talking. That was one way of dealing with it, I guess.

The pillar of smoke seemed to wave to us from over the trees. Demonic and churning. Taunting. We rowed back in a hurry.

It was the church. Of course it was. The wives trapped inside. Impossible but you just knew: we had been left alone for too long. Then Krylov's wife came running up the path. They both fell to their knees and held each other, *thankyoulordjesus* and all that when really it was just the little bitch's laziness, sleeping in while the other wives went to church, while the other wives burned, leaving their husbands standing and staring, framed by flames, *herelordjesusismyeverlastingenmity*. I was just grateful my own wife had been taken away long ago, in that other life before I was sent here, and was now safely tucked away in some other man's bed. Or at least I could hope. When I looked at the other scientists I could see they were destroyed. Since my cabin was closest, I went to get the vodka.

The wives died in a suffocated heap. The ones on the bottom were not as badly burned, still looked like something, like dolls maybe, at the edge of a rubbish fire. We laid them out on the ground, passed the bottle between us, the scientists cried and moaned and held their awful wife-corpses. So blank so quickly. Vlasov was the worst: shaking violently, shivering snot-ropes spilling from his face. Then the sky sounded its artillery, turned dark, opened up. Heavy smashing rain, exploding in the forest around us, ground gone mud. I took charge. We buried them right then and there. Borisov made four crosses out of rough sticks bound at the middle, little ones like for children, it was the best that could be done, we were all getting very drunk. Luckily, I knew the Twenty-third Psalm by heart.

"That's good," Krylov said, wiping his hand across his mouth.

"What's good about it?" I snapped. I could feel the others seeing him now. "Just take your wife home!" I shouted. Shouldn't have said that word. He hauled her away. Krylov's wife looked back at me over her shoulder. Rain-pasted hair wrapped her face, cold skin just to look at, like frozen flowers, those bleach-stained lips. "Everyone go back to your own cabins!" I ordered, and stood there and waited, watching them shuffle along their separate paths.

In my dreams I am young and planning to go to film school when my boxing career is over. Such things were still possible back then. Sometimes I still played the director in my mind, it was a way of framing life. On the lake that day it was all long, fluid shots, *thisisonetake* I would whisper, big light flattened around us, quiet and tense. And then the fiery tails in the sky, cue soaring music, surreal cinema like falling dragons, some storming the lake but most streaking away from us, God putting on his show, whistles and crashing echoes in the forest for accompaniment, then falling off, the denouement settling in as the air turned crushed chalk. Then we saw the crooked pile of smoke. Then the day fell to pieces. Quick cuts, everything too visceral, I edited dead wives tightly with my eyes, harder and harder, all night long, drinking and smoking until I passed out in my chair.

Morning. Cabin cold floor. Teeth hurt more than usual. Made a fire, some coffee, lit a cigar. Watching smoke. Hard to think about thinking. My story now, how it would go.

Things would get very bad very quickly, that much was sure. The scientists might talk like civilized men but soon this would mean nothing. Their extended families had been taken by the Revolution and the War. Then the Boss took their children, holding onto them like chips in a poker game, *keepplayingorelse*. He let them have their wives just to sweeten the pot. And then the vast forest, this immense nothingness, and internal exile, and waiting for the game to resume. But now four shallow graves had ruined that game. Now it was last hand. These guys could only take so many bad beats.

I went outside to the big tree, to hit the heavy bag for a while. Breathing short snorts of steam, lungs hurting from smoking too much, reminded me of the ring, the way smaller men always tried to come inside on you, banging away at your ribs, punching your air out. You had to get ahold of them, take away their space, then push them away and knock them down from a distance. Little bastards, not so smart then.

Vlasov would go first. Having a young, pretty wife was great stuff until you had to hold her blackened corpse. Poor girl; she'd been a true believer, the kind who volunteers for the front of the parade, so the Boss volunteered her to be Vlasov's wife. It actually made her happy. For a time Vlasov was a star, a state hero, one of the scientists who had worked on SCAR and WELT and the ZARR machines, and all those cobalt rockets that blew up on the launch pad, until the Boss got frustrated and bored and decided to put him away for a while, like a child putting away a toy, only this box was a freezing cabin at the northern edge of nowhere, somewhere between exile and erasure. Vlasov's wife never complained. The pact was made. Somehow love remained. While everyone else tried to be detached from their fate, expecting the worst in the end, it was Vlasov, small and spectacled and awkward in his oversized suits, who still went into the woods to pick his wife flowers, who held her hand as they wandered the shore together. They were the youngest. They had only lost one child. They could still imagine things.

"Just another day for you, eh No-No?"

I didn't turn around. Two years in his company and I knew Petrov's voice like old cuts in my face. "The scientist formerly known as Petrov," I grunted, hooking a low blow to the bag. That was the official greeting, something that was only used sarcastically in this place.

"Oh yes, that's good, No-No. Just business as usual, eh? Just another day."

I stopped and held the bag still, looked to the ground. "No, not just another day, Petrov. I am truly sorry about your wife."

Petrov: oldest, most ruined. Piss in his eyes, no one left but a fat wife who complained bitterly about her diminished circumstances, no books and too much drink after supper. He always said that somewhere there was a firing squad using my picture for target practice. Petrov: there were times when I did feel sorry for him. Now was one of them. Now his fat wife was dead. Now he was drunk off his feet, waving a bottle around.

"Hey No-No, thanks a lot. Trouble is, I don't give a shit. I don't care what you think. You think you can give *me* sympathy? You think you're in a better place? Guess again, brother. You're deluding yourself. Someday they're going to come for you ..."

I punched him the face. Not too hard, just square in the mouth. Went right down. Drunks fall better, no flailing around. What he said wasn't true. I wasn't deluding myself. The burnt-out church was just a hundred yards away.

Petrov sputtered blood from his lips, tried to lift his head. Couldn't. His eyes opened up to the sky above. "You have to radio for more wives," he said. "The Boss will parachute them in over the lake, he'll send them with the next supplies." He tried to pour vodka into his mouth, spilled it all over his neck. "Hell," he laughed, "it'll be exciting."

Raining again. I went inside to make breakfast. When I came back out with an extra cup of coffee, Petrov was gone.

The radio had its own windowless shed, a padlock the size of a fist. I had the only key. Locked the door from the inside, sat down with candle and bottle. Petrov and his idea: my idea now. Six cigarettes later I knew what to send.

ALL WIVES BURNED IN FIRE STOP NO OTHER CASUALTIES STOP REQUEST NEW WIVES STOP REQUEST FIVE WIVES STOP PLEASE SEND FIVE WIVES WITH NEXT DROP STOP PLEASE PARA-CHUTE WIVES WITH NEXT DROP STOP

No reply unless an emergency. This was not an emergency. They would either send the women or no. The beginning or the end.

The Boss would think about this one, chew it and smoke it and play with it over dinner.

Met him once: right before my last fight, came into my dressing room and stood just outside the cone of overhead light. Not a big man at all but shadow filled the space all behind him, blotted his bodyguards into the background.

I moved to get up from the table where the trainer was working on my shoulders. A white glove waved me down. "Are you ready to do what you have to do, Brother Nonolovsky?"

So strange to hear that voice so close, no radio static around it. And before I could answer he was leaving the room.

None of the scientists had ever met the Boss. To them he was like cancer or the devil. Now they spent all their time cursing him, damning everything. Life around the camp virtually stopped. I thought about confiscating their liquor. It was too cruel.

I did the rounds. I stocked their wood and built their fires. Made them get out of bed long enough to change their clothes. Forced them to eat something. Sat and smoked with them, shrugged and looked away from them. Put them to bed. They didn't argue. The pistol on my hip was beside the point. The shotgun was hidden, wrapped in plastic, sleeping in a tree not far from my cabin.

Vomit down the front of his shirt, sitting in his own piss and shit, drunk beyond thought, abusive and violent one minute, hopelessly despondent the next: this was Petrov. Had to knock him around a little. Pushed down into the oversized washtub that doubled as a bath, he crouched and cringed and asked me about his idea. "Hey asshole, did you radio for the new wives yet?" I said I was thinking about it, made him promise not to say anything to the others. "I haven't seen anyone in days," he said, spitting out soap.

Sitting in the cold and dark, a hunched-over lump, grey upon grey, unresponsive: Borisov. Not drinking at all. An army of spiders crawled over the floor. I needed to get him out of that cabin. "You have to help me with the next air-drop," I told him.

Every morning putting fresh flowers on his wife's grave, constantly crying, sagging as if broken, his face a blotch of pain: Vlasov. But at least his clothes were clean. "You have to help me with the next air-drop," I told him.

Anxious, bewildered, ashamed, compulsive movements, obsessive thoughts, dirty and unshaven and smoking instead of eating, no sleep: Simonov. Weakest. All the music of failure – with its past accompaniment of broken bones, drilled teeth, fractured backs – was nothing now. An empty nightshirt. Forced him to drink half a bottle with me, made him lie down while I sat there and waited for him to fall asleep.

Constantly fucking his wife: Krylov. Had to pound on the door and stand there and wait. *Idiot.* His embarrassment distasteful to look at, paranoid and babbling in an attempt to reassure himself. "How are the others? Are they taking it hard? Still, I should stay away, shouldn't I? Let them deal with their grief? They're not angry at me, are they? My wife was spared, they should be glad for that. We're safe, aren't we? These are educated men, they're not going to do anything crazy, are they? Should I worry about Petrov?"

I told him to shut up and stay inside with his door locked. I told him I was taking care of things. "The next supplies might help," I said. Krylov's wife moved around in the background. She seemed taller, her dress tighter across her breasts.

I lost my own wife when I lost my last fight. Shouldn't have lost either. True, the Nigerian was very quick: all smiles and cool business like he was snatching at flies, dancing then *flickflickflick*. He was beautiful, really. But I could have destroyed him. And yet: my right hand would just not go. I kept waiting for it to go. I waited too long. It was like the thought was stuck in my mind, jamming the order to my arm. I lost by decision.

The captain who came to arrest me also delivered the divorce papers. He was older. It was better to get the older guys; the young guys believed in their uniforms too much.

He said he was sorry. I was sorry, too. It was ten years in a labour camp, then here to guard the little men and their wives. No wife for me. Here was awful but better.

The day of the air-drop arrived. I took Vlasov and Borisov with me. Borisov was hard to rouse, that scrap-paper stare, I had to push him into his clothes. Vlasov was nervous and distracted. I sat at the back while the two of them rowed us out into the middle of the lake. They knew the drill. I said nothing.

Sun high and middle, light scattered and reflecting around. The plane appeared out of the south, made two passes before spilling its cargo. Usually there was just one chute, maybe two around a holiday, but now there were four floating in the sky. I thought I could see the kick of legs, that distinctive tell of a human shape. But only from one of them.

"What the hell?" Vlasov muttered.

I said nothing. I was just as confused. The plane disappeared. We rowed around the bend in the lake, over to where the chutes came down. Behind trees. We were jerking through the water, Vlasov kept missing the pace. I got things ready, untangled the ropes and hooks.

There were three floating crates and one floating human being. We went to the human being first. He was calm and smiling. "Over here, brothers!" he called happily, waving an arm. He had shed his harness in the water, the chute spread out behind him like a wet cloud.

He grabbed the side of the boat with both hands. He was young, blonde, good looking. A former athlete. Only athletes had teeth like that.

"Who are you?" Vlasov asked, his voice pitched.

The man laughed. "I'm Major Topilin, of course. And who are you, brother, who asks such direct questions, and how waterlogged do I have to be before you fellows pull me in? There's war on the eastern front, your country needs you, you're going to be rehabilitated, you're going to work on the Protean Machine, I'm here to get you ready to evacuate in two weeks time."

I shot him in the neck. It was very loud. Vlasov jumped straight up, electrified. I put a bullet through his heart. He fell over like a tree, tumbling into the water. Borisov just looked at me. "Hurry up," he growled.

I left the three bodies in the lake. I had to pry Major Topilin's fingers away from the boat. If he said two weeks I probably had five or six days. It was not easy rowing back with three crates in tow. I thought about that skin on the inside of thighs. My brain was working perfectly. My stomach was churning. No one met me at the shore. The sun went down as

I hauled the last crate in. All three crates were filled with crosses, eleven of them, carved in the old style, an angel over each name. I hammered the lids back into place.

I met Petrov on the path. He was not too drunk now, looked better than he had for a week. "Hey No-No, did you radio for the new wives yet?"

"I did," I answered.

Petrov was surprised. "You asshole! Did they radio back?"

The light was failing, the smell of leaves and earth taking over. "Not out here," I said. "Let's talk in my cabin."

I stuffed Petrov's body into an old water barrel. No encouragement for wolves. When I reached into the tree I found the shotgun was gone. I knew who had it but I had to see Simonov first.

Simonov was dead in his bunk. He had written some pages denouncing his own role in various projects, asked forgiveness for dressing up death as science, *same old, same old*. I took some cigarettes and left. I was getting so hungry, I could almost smell her hair.

With one grunt I kicked in Krylov's front door. Inside in a flash. I had a rope in one hand and a pistol in the other. Krylov had my shotgun but he was not the creature to use it, you could see the idea stuck there in his face. Then I started looking at *her*. I had five or six days.

in the kingdom
of chicken

In this kingdom, she thought, *I make the chicken*. Somewhere in the back of a blue-lined book, on an antique telephone table in a hallway across town, was her name and phone number and the word *chicken*. And when that name was pressed with a finger and half whispered out loud, her phone would ring and she would be invited to a dinner party. The married voice on the other end would talk in a hurry about how busy they'd both been and how bad it was that they hadn't seen each other more and how that would have to change, "Starting now, we're having some of our single friends over for dinner and you just have to come, I insist. You can bring your fabulous chicken."

The recipe book called it Indian Chicken Curry, golden slick and gleaming in its photograph but when asked (by new people, these strangers this year) she said it was "just chicken." Everyone said how delicious it was and made the appropriate noises, and while she could hear them and see how their mouths moved (how could she not, all chairs pushed together under one Chinese lantern, all hot shadows and elbows careful), it all felt like something careless and thick and rubbery inside, how hard she worked for these promised white moments that arrived instead like something pink and skinned and quivering. Sometimes she didn't know what the hell she was doing, just who she was trying to please, these faces so close around the table made it hard for her to breathe, especially this man across from her who just sat there and smiled, this man she had been introduced to so his name could fall right out of her head two minutes later, this tall, blonde man with his tight, shy mouth.

Here and there, in little glances, she watched him eat. She had done this before, with other men. Sometimes it made her happy too, there was something simple and physical and human about it, this thing about eating together, especially about a woman watching a man enjoy food, seeing his satisfaction, this man's lips moving like an inside joke, like a secret story. After dinner she could walk right up and put her hand on his arm and that secret would fly right out of him, men never knew what to do when you did that. And then she would have him. Her hand could push and pull at him however she liked, he would have no more sense than a kite.

They would have a connection then – tethered together for moments of close focus, wet eyes staring, a kiss in the kitchen, in the car, in the park, telling her how fantastic she was, that voice in her ear, on her neck, those weeks where everything is said with your hands, he would push her down and push up her knees and look up at her with his face like a furnace, greedily from between her legs, telling her how great she tasted, her hands in his damp hair to say *what are you doing, what are you doing to me*, it would be something to hold onto, to hold in her head, to feed her in those empty moments while driving or watching television when there was nothing on or sitting there at lunch pushing a fork around, not eating at all, looking around to see if anyone was watching her, so conscious she was of her person these days, the way her body couldn't be trusted, trying but always tired, making her late, she'd come home from work to see her face fixed hard with lines, stand there in an ugly sleepiness, not knowing what to do with herself, not wanting to do anything except take a nap, on the couch so she'd still have her bed to go to later on, wake up sweaty and sick, swearing *tomorrow will be better*, she had a list and the alarm set for five a.m, she'd get up early and exercise, every day, if she could just lose tenfifteentwenty pounds, in the meantime she'd keep that list taped to the mirror, paint the bathroom, tile the kitchen, finish the book, the yard, the basement, maybe even plan that trip with her sister, and she'd get new glasses too, and some new clothes, and then steal into the realm of this blonde man and take all his princely power, and this time she'd keep it too, and be free, so she wouldn't have to sit starving in this other once-a-year kingdom, as flimsy as a leper's tent, thinking *Next year you bastards, next year I'll be ready and I'll have you in my jaws.*

how to read cards

Chixi-Shin dealt the future face-up, three cards at a time. It was the work of seeing and believing. It was like looking for weather without having windows, like carrying crosses without any prayer. Yet the basics were simple: Hearts were water, Clubs were fire, Diamonds were earth, Spades were air. Individual cards had further meanings, and between all of them they could cover an entire life's sky, every sun and cloud and wind and rain, from love to money to health to luck.

Chixi-Shin tried to be careful with the cards, turning them over only when she needed to. Recent weeks, however, had forced her hand. All at once her job had become unbearable. Chixi-Shin worked at the Ministry for Punishing Ugly Children but it felt like she hardly worked at all anymore. The problem was her office-mate, Tai Kao. He had found a new friend. Chixi-Shin called her *the Incredible Talking Lady*. Tai Kao was a killer, and Chixi-Shin respected the hell out of him for that, but she did not understand how he could have such unlimited patience for this pushy woman and her endless visits. Yes, the Incredible Talking Lady had been recently widowed, and yes, Tai Kao was lonely too, but couldn't they just get on with it instead of all this talking? Whole afternoons went by, wasted away, the Incredible Talking Lady standing there, twitching at his cubicle door, all noise and teeth and thin hips and tossing blond hair, and Tai Kao with his horribly awkward smile, watching her lips with his one yellow eye. It was oppressive, impossible to get anything done. The paperwork piled up. Many ugly children went unpunished. Worst of all (because it came to her as a surprise), Chixi-Shin felt hurt and ignored.

She turned to the cards. They confirmed her darkest ideas and promised much worse: the Queen of Diamonds symbolized the fair-haired woman, the disturber, the gossip; Six of Diamonds was bad news like arrows, a descending death, rushing to earth, leading to separation and loss; Three of Spades was the pig card, where the relationship swells and breaks, and a third party is responsible.

The knowledge made Chixi-Shin distracted and anxious. She had a stomachache all the time. Every morning she stood for long minutes before her office building, reluctant to go in, watching people climb the steps, imagining thought-bubbles over their heads like *I want to go swimming soon* and *I don't care what she thinks* and *My head feels funny* and *I think I'm dying*. On the front sidewalk someone had spray-painted the words TEETH=YES! in two-foot tall, neon-orange letters. The Incredible Talking Lady continued her bottomless visits. Her capacity for chatter was mind numbing. For his own part, Tai Kao started coming to work with combed hair and a pressed uniform. He wore clean, white gloves over his red, angry-looking hands. Chixi-Shin felt awkward, found it difficult to look at him. She went for fake walks around the department, pretended to have quiet moments by large windows. *Parading my big bum around*, she thought. Were people watching her? Tai Kao and the Incredible Talking Lady seemed to take no notice. They continued with their unconsummated foolishness, the pretending and prelude without end. *Please just do it already*, Chixi-Shin prayed. That would shut them up.

And then suddenly, mercifully, they were both incinerated in the first firebombings that spring. It was the beginning of the Great Emergency.

At first Chixi-Shin felt vindicated. Released. Here was proof; the future was all around her, all she had to do was see it, feel it, read it. It was in the air, vibrations like ringing, barely heard, an invisible quivering, barely there. She could imagine its waves in perfect black lines, radiating concentric arcs like in a school film from the fifties (*The Wonder of Radio* perhaps, or *Earthquakes Explained*), a spreading energy sweeping out to reach her, the pulse *there*, and *there*, she could watch it waver and wash over. *Positive-negative ionic molecular fields*, she sometimes explained but there was, in fact, no scientific basis for this. It just made people feel better. Which was at the heart of it, after all. The human element. Because this approaching future (like all things, Chixi-Shin knew) had a feeling inside of it, encrypted, wired to it through and through. And yet the feeling of this new, approaching future, this particular future, was mostly a matter of ache, of something long and tired and wasted in hateful misery. Which turned her blue inside, made her feel defeated and empty.

The bombs continued to fall in their neat black patterns. There were napalm attacks, air attacks, incendiary attacks, cluster bombings, fire raids, saturation bombings and various liquidation maneuvers. The Ministry for Punishing Ugly Children, along with the city around it, disappeared in a gigantic firestorm. Everyone fled into the wilderness of the open roads.

The trouble with fleeing was that it was incredibly boring. Yes, it was a relief to find oxygen, and sure, Chixi-Shin hoped the exercise might reduce the size of her bum, but very quickly the road flattened you out, spilled out your will to live, because everything just went on and on. People ran, and their thoughts ran with them, until their brains clicked down to somewhere between empty and static. Chixi-Shin imagined thought-bubbles over the heads of her fellow travellers, things like *I must get away from my stinky feet* and *Where can I buy some lottery tickets?* and *I think these people are following me*. But distractions were not enough. She was too tired; she could not go on. She spread out a blanket in a ditch beside the road and turned over three more cards: the Eight of Spades signalled the mountains of a mighty enemy, danger and upset and darkness falling; the King of Spades marked the emergence of a dark-haired, ambitious man, a mystery and saviour; the Six of Hearts meant sudden good luck, travel to a better place, possibly because of the interest and efforts of another. This, and the fact that she had on her favourite iridescent pearl raincoat, made Chixi-Shin feel almost happy again, and she decided to wait there and see what happened.

People going by exclaimed all sorts of things, especially in mangled German, things like *Schlechte Bomben!* (Bad bombs!) and *Fliehen Sie!* (Flee!) and *Durchlauf weg!* (Run away!) and *Ich verdiene es!* (I deserve it!). Some stopped to sit with Chixi-Shin and complain about their troubles. But the Great Emergency had not yet acquired the full dimensions of language, and many lacked the proper tools to express themselves. Certainly they had terror fatigue, body-count fatigue and ordnance fatigue, and many were brain-blasted and awed beyond belief. Chixi-Shin ate her sandwiches and listened. Everyone was searching for reasons. Some said the war was propagated by the barbarian princes, started over the right to succession, but if you believed that then you deserved all the hellfire bombings that were surely coming your way. No, it was about music, and what the people would listen to until the end of time, and who would decide that. The barbarian princes paraded the decorum and etiquette of *li*, swooned with the humanity and love of *jen*, and lusted for the appropriately classical themes of empire: Beethoven's *Symphony Number Five*, Schubert's *Death and the Maiden*, Hadyn's *Lord Nelson Mass*, Verdi's *Messa Da Requiem*, and *La Damnation de Faust* by Berlioz. Opposing them was the Wu Wan King, somewhere in the northern mountains, remote but lurking over everything. Armed with his *t'en ming* – the mandate of heaven – his aim was simple: he just wanted to rock you. Until the matter was decided, roadside loudspeakers would only alternate between static crackling and the whine of jammed signals. It was a horrible noise.

After many days Chixi-Shin grew restless and tired of sandwiches. She was just about to resume her wanderings when a rider came up. His long blonde hair trailed out of his helmet. With a beautiful smile he handed Chixi-Shin a tube containing a letter, then spurred his horse and raced away. *Ah letter,* Chixi-Shin thought, *you are the ground marked out for anticipation.* The letter read:

Dear Nice Girl Chixi-Shin,

I call you that because that is the way my dear son Tai Kao often made little references to you in his letters. Always he was a good son and wrote me many letters in fine humour, many times he sent me little presents, and always he told me how much he loved me. You probably did not know that, did you, Chixi-Shin? Most people would not suspect that. Most people would be surprised. Yes, he was a decorated war hero, killer of many men with his bare hands, but he was also very sweet and soft inside, especially to his dear mother. Also, he was very lonely. Because people were afraid of him. That eye-patch made him look mean.

I have his letters and presents all around me but still I cannot stop crying all day and all night, my misery heart is dark and broken and I hope very much that you never have to feel something so bad, it is a terrible force that has propagated this hateful war and no music in all the known world will ever be able to fix me inside, I miss my dear son so very, very much. So if there is anything you can tell me about my dear, dear Tai Kao, anything at all, it would be so much comfort to a poor grieving mother. If you could tell me anything at all about the friends he had, I never wanted to ask him because I feared the answer and I feared for his loneliness and I wondered if he would ever find a kind woman to settle down with but now I think maybe he was just secretive and I should never have worried. One can hope. He often mentioned you favourably, said you were a good and quiet and dependable person to work with, and nice to talk to, so I hope you can write down a few lines for a poor grieving mother who loved her son so very much.

I have nothing to look forward to when I look at the door anymore.

I will pray for your soul every day,

Helga Kao

PS – Do not worry so much about the size of your bum. I'm sure you are very lovely.

Chixi-Shin turned away from the letter in her lap. She looked around at the people prostrating themselves in the fields along the road, how they prayed and listened close to the ground for the strains of heavenly music. All this purity of motive, all these individuals like planets of revolving will, trying to orientate themselves to the shifting forces of a dynamic future. Understanding this was the key to everything, that was one way to look at it. Then there was the other: the motion of the stars fixed, their trajectories already known. In this view there was nothing dynamic at all, only destiny and fate, the cards of love, money, health, luck turned over long before. Here the future could be gathered in pieces if one read things the right way, if one surrendered to the proper questions, and sought truthful answers. The prize of knowledge was everything. The people of Wan could pray all they wanted, but their destinies might have been determined long ago. What was Chixi-Shin supposed to say to this poor woman? She certainly didn't want to say anything. The very idea made her nauseous.

Chixi-Shin went back to wandering. She hoped it would help her think. It didn't. There were antipersonnel operations going on to the south and vengeance raids going on to the west, so the roads were charged with people in various states of shock. Every once in a while some soldiers would appear and order people into columns. There were slave marches, forced marches and evacuation marches. Chixi-Shin took care to avoid them all. She still had some sandwiches left.

It was difficult to think with people screaming all the time, with bawling young mothers trying to give their babies away. The landscape was equally distracting; there was so much collateral damage, so much charred wreckage with the haunted qualities of fire-blackened dinosaurs and bombed submarines. Maybe it was the end of the world. There were only so many people left to euthanize.

But a night in the forest with the cards told a different story. The Five of Spades – although called the "coffin card" – meant only temporary obstacles, some minor troubles, or negative personalities, whose power to cause disruption was entirely within one's control. The Eight of Hearts signified a gift or a visit or some flattery or an invitation. And the Nine of Hearts, the wish card, was potentially very good, the dream revealed like an unfurled flag, but only to those willing to take it up. Chixi-Shin laid her blanket out on the forest floor, pulled her jacket over her, and went to sleep smiling.

She awoke to another messenger emerging from the morning trees. He had shining black hair. He carried an official offer from the Wu Wan King himself, his imperial seal gorgeous in its thick glob of wax. Chixi-Shin did not hesitate. She made her way back to the main road, traded her last sandwiches for a putt-putt scooter, and sputtered north along muddy country lanes to her new job.

It was a teaching position at the Ministry of Seeing, Learning and Knowing, otherwise known as the Department of Responsibility. It was a good job. Besides, she was tired of all the fleeing and hellfire killing. The Great Emergency had forced everyone to rethink their priorities. She arrived at the

Ministry late at night. She was shown to a small room with a sink, a toilet, a dresser and a single bed. The dresser was full of uniforms. Soon a soldier came with a bowl of hot soup. Chixi-Shin was quite content. Before she went to sleep she laid out three cards. The first card was the Jack of Diamonds, which signalled the appearance of strange men, up to five of them, with unknown motives. The second card was the Five of Hearts, which warned of jealousy and ill will from others. And the third card was the Four of Spades, a card like an uncaring shrug because it meant worries, problems and personal lows. Still, Chixi-Shin remained hopeful for the future.

The next morning she was awakened by a Captain Woo. He took her to a classroom in the east wing. It contained five men chained to their desks. Chixi-Shin immediately recognized them as the Pitbull Generals. She had seen their faces on dozens of posters; before the Great Emergency they had comprised the trusted inner circle of the Wu Wan Kingdom. But then the barbarian princes tempted them with money and talented women, and promised them great power, so that they tried to stage a coup.

"These men are traitors," said Captain Woo. "They have tried to overthrow the government and failed. It is your job to make them understand their responsibility. They must write a letter of contrition. You have one month. Good luck."

The Pitbull Generals were named You-Ta, Zhang-Ta, Kong-Ta, Jien-Ta and Fan-Ta. But they were all pretty much interchangeable. They all had fearsomely big heads and wild wet eyes. They had each attempted various forms of suicide – "manipulative, self-injurious behaviour," Captain Woo called it – and each had the wince-inducing scars and speckled rope-burns to show for it. Now they sat hunched in their desks, miserable and growling. Randomly, eruptively, they would throw their enormous heads down, sobbing and tearing at their closely shaved beards.

Chixi-Shin realized she had been given an immensely important task. She needed to proceed cautiously. Carefully.

Standing there at the front of the classroom, she worried that the size of her bum made her look ridiculous. She decided to start simply and directly. In a polite, conversational voice, Chixi-Shin asked the Pitbull Generals to talk about their responsibility. *Why did you plot against the government? What did you hope to accomplish?* She wrote her questions across the chalkboard in neat, inviting cursive. But the Pitbull Generals would only moan and weep.

The next day was just as unpromising. In the courtyard next door they were executing dentists, and the noise was maddening. Strangely, the generals became quiet and calm. Chixi-Shin shut all the windows. The room grew very warm with the heat from the generals' heads. She stood before them and cried. "Please, please," she sobbed, "admit your responsibility." They stared back at her like she was a little blue fish swimming along the bottom of the ocean. She continued to plead for three days.

Time got very bumpy. It was a gruelling type of existence. Chixi-Shin had no fun and no one to talk to. As if to remind her of that, the vending machines in the bathrooms offered only aspirin, never condoms or candy. None of the mirrors seemed to work properly. She rubbed her eyes a lot. Everywhere there were signs that said, *Remember! You are at the mercy of your teacher!* but she hardly felt in control of anything. Her life-force felt more like the sign on the electric fence, which read DO NOT TOUCH ME OR I WILL HURT YOU. Further up the mountain was a debtor's prison, where they were always screaming and disturbing the morning air. The loudspeakers randomly rattled and racketed to life, but only with nonsensical sound. And every night there were bombing raids in the distance. Chixi-Shin overheard two officers joke that the Wu Wan King could only fall asleep to the gentle whistle of falling bombs.

Every day Chixi-Shin woke up determined to do her job. She tried increasingly radical strategies to make her charges talk. She made them watch films with titles like *Lions Take*

Down Baby Elephant, *Tiger Turns On Trainer*, and *Dogs Chasing Children*. She shouted and barked at them for hours on end. She handed out Frequently-Asked-Question sheets: *What is the most effective form of torture? Does torture work? How long do torture sessions last? Do people ever recover from torture?* The generals, however, grew quieter and quieter.

Finally, exasperated, she invited them to talk about anything they wanted. *I mean it!* she wrote on the board. Their tongues were thick and awkward, but what was at first a few mumbles quickly became boisterous. For whole days they talked about weather and tactics and all the great painters, especially the German Expressionists. Once they had a subject in their teeth, they could be relentlessly tenacious; Zhang-Ta, for example, spent an entire afternoon explaining and defending his position that Styx's *Mr. Roboto* was the most overblown song ever.

Chixi-Shin did not join their conversations. She had no desire; mostly she just felt cold. Their words poured over and over her. She imagined icons floating over their heads: a bomb, a fire, a star, a sword, a banana. One night Captain Woo came to see her. "You have one week left," he said. "But don't worry; in the meantime, I have doubled your ration of soup."

Chixi-Shin turned to the cards. Four of Clubs: dishonesty and deceit; the key to the situation is temporarily lost. Ace of Spades: the card of swords; misfortune and death. Ten of Hearts: good luck and success after much difficulty. *Domo arigato!* she cried. The road would be hard but she still might succeed. She was very grateful for the chance.

The next morning Chixi-Shin wrote the proposed subject of a letter on the blackboard: *Why It Is Bad To Try To Overthrow The Government*. Each of the generals would write their own part, their own measure of guilt, in turn, one after the other, on the same piece of paper (the Wu Wan King did not have the patience to read multiple pages).

The generals smiled back at her. They seemed amenable. She found herself holding her breath as she watched them write and then pass the paper along.

Why It Is Bad To Try To Overthrow The Government

Dearest Wu Wan King,
It is bad to try to overthrow the government. Why?
Because often your co-conspirators are less than competent. Only when you realize that You-Ta has not
gotten his tanks into the capital by noon, that Zhang-
Ta has not secured the airport, that Kong-Ta has not
seized the radio stations, and that Jien-Ta has let the
Minister of Truth slip away, only then does one realize that people cannot be counted on, and how bad it
is to try to overthrow the government.
Your Loyal Servant,
Fan-Ta

Dearest Wu Wan King,
It is bad to try to overthrow the government. Very
bad. Why is it so bad? Because you have to rely on unreliable people. It is one thing to make promises, quite
another to actually keep them. So when You-Ta does
not get his tanks into the capital by noon, when
Zhang-Ta does not secure the airport, when Kong-Ta
does not take over the radio stations, and when Fan-
Ta does not take Your Person into custody (and dispose of your guard), that is when one comes to grieve
over the unreliability of so-called friends, and how
bad it is to try to overthrow the government.
Regretfully,
Jien-Ta

Dearest Wu Wan King,
It is bad to try to overthrow the government. A big
mistake. Why is it such a mistake? Because the mistakes of others will doom you to failure. What use is
it to seize all the radio stations when You-Ta does not
get his tanks into the capital by noon, when Zhang-Ta

does not secure the airport, when Jien-Ta lets the Minister of Truth get away, when Fan-Ta does not take Your Person into custody (and execute your guard)? No number of radio stations can help you then, when you finally realize how bad it is to try to overthrow the government.
Regretfully,
Kong-Ta

Dearest Wu Wan King,
It is bad to try to overthrow the government. Call it a tragedy. Why is it such a tragedy? Because trust is misplaced, and a man's weakness will bring his ruin and yours. You-Ta did not get his tanks into the capital by noon. Kong-Ta failed to seize the radio stations. Jien-Ta let the Minister of Truth escape arrest. Fan-Ta did not imprison Your Person (and shoot all your guards). By then it was useless to take over the airport. Why disrupt the travel plans of so many hopeful people? *They* know how bad it is to try to overthrow the government; why should they be punished by ruining their holidays?
Considerately,
Zhang-Ta

Dearest Wu Wan King,
It is bad to try to overthrow the government. Why? Because so much depends on timing, and life does not always cooperate. I had to get my tanks into the capital by noon. But I overslept. You see, it was my daughter's wedding the night before. Perhaps I had too much to drink. I am very sorry. But then again, Zhang-Ta did not secure the airport, and Kong-Ta failed to seize the radio stations, and Jien-Ta let the Minister of Truth slip out a back door, and Fan-Ta did not imprison Your Person (and feed your guard to

wild dogs). So I should not be too hard on myself. Obviously, others are to blame as well. And that itself explains why it is bad to overthrow the government.
Wiser Now,
You-Ta

Failure. Chixi-Shin went back to her room for the rest of the day. That night, in a dream, Chixi-Shin saw all the known world bombarded with musical notes. Filling the heavens. And the notes were like heavy razors, because they fell straight and quick, and cut people down where they struck them. The next morning she knew what to do.

Captain Woo had to seek special permission, but within a few hours Chixi-Shin was allowed to proceed. Soldiers set up a stereo and speakers in her classroom. The Pitbull Generals grew very afraid. The soldiers exited hurriedly, like servants who had just fed a bad meal to a cranky emperor. Chixi-Shin pressed "Play." The first strains of "All Out of Love" by Air Supply filled the room. The effect was like poison gas.

Chixi-Shin still had to threaten them with a Bryan Adams recording, but very quickly it was all over. Within fifteen minutes the generals had composed a simple note:

Wu Wan King.
Come on.
Forgive us.
Be quick.
We are sorry.

p.s. – We are sorry.

Everyone was very moved, including Chixi-Shin. Soldiers in chemical outfits came and took away the stereo. The Pitbull Generals hugged each other over and over again. Immense tears streamed down the faces of their giant heads. Soldiers wearing white gloves brought in a five-layered chocolate cake. The generals gathered round with linked arms and took turns singing verses of "Rocket Man" before blowing out the dozens of candles. The icing was decorated to say: *Congratulations Pit Bull Generals!* It was a delicious cake.

The next day the generals were taken out and shot. Standing on the balcony over the courtyard, staring down at the odd postures of their broken bodies, Chixi-Shin could not help but feel a little sad. But then the loudspeakers all crackled to life, and "Fat-Bottomed Girls" by Queen came on, and that was awesome.

an arsonist's guide to physics

It was an exam in physics in the eleventh grade. There was nine of us. There was always nine of us, all the way through. The entire school was a hundred kids at most, kindergarten to grade twelve. It was 1985 in Saskatchewan.

I was the only town kid in my class. The rest all came from farms. They were like brothers and sisters who spoke a different language. They had chores with chickens and cattle. I had a paper route and an unwritten contract with any old lady who wanted her lawn mowed or her weeds pulled for five dollars and a can of warm pop. Sometimes I had a bike but mostly I lived on my feet, the town wasn't so much houses and streets as it was a series of shortcuts and a list that kept on ticking.

For the first nine years the farm kids lived and died by how close they sat to the back of their long, orange bus. Then they got cars. By the end of high school they talked about the family operation, how they were getting screwed by the government or the weather. Their fathers were in the business of propaganda. My dad was a guy who laid on the floor in his pajamas all day. He liked the French channel. The words were only noise but he said there was nothing else on.

Every day I walked to school and every day the principal was waiting for me. He was like a stock character from a bad movie: short-sleeved business shirt, pocket protector, clip-on tie, thick plastic glasses, pencil moustache and hair combed back in straight Brylcreem lines. If I was more than five minutes late he'd stand there with his watch held out, telling me to turn around. He was the first boss to give me days off for bad behaviour.

The principal was also our physics teacher. He taught most of the subjects I hated: algebra, calculus, geo-trig. In a parent-teacher interview where my mom kept looking at the ceiling, I half sold him on the idea that these subjects were simply boring me. Really I just didn't have the brain for it; I'd rather memorize the life of every English king than even try to understand sine and cosine.

Still, the physics exam we had that day in the eleventh grade wasn't much of a disaster; I'd probably scored a mid-sixty. The real trouble came from the timing. It was the period before lunch, and when the bell rang and the exam was over, the principal gathered up the papers and stacked them on the desk at the front and then looked at his watch and up at the clock and just walked out, *leaving the exams behind*.

Everyone was looking at everyone else but I couldn't stick around – an hour only gave me just enough time to get home and jostle for position with my six brothers and sisters, scarf down lunch and turn around again. It was soup bowls in a line, a pile of sandwiches in the middle. Being fast meant getting seconds. This day I was fast but instead I used the time to get back to school.

The classroom was empty. The pile of exams was stacked more neatly than before.

I knew they'd been at it – nothing too obvious of course, just everyone helping themselves to a grade or two. Now no one wanted to be anywhere near the scene of the crime. I looked at the clock. The bell would go off in less than ten minutes.

As usual, the decision was made by my feet. I walked up to the desk and stuffed that pile of exams into my duffel bag, under some books. I put the bag on the back shelf, where I always put it. Then I went to wash my hands.

No one came back until just after the bell. Everyone assumed the principal had retrieved the exams. For the principal's part – as he loudly explained to us while tearing apart our classroom two days later – he didn't even realize the exams were missing until the next time he saw the word *physics* in his weekly planner. And that was far too late to save them from the burning barrel I incinerated them in, their orange light refracted and dancing in the back of my eye.

death of a
dictator

The dictator is dead. His people – and he would call them that, even now – are rejoicing. Especially in the Christian south, they dance and sing and spit gleeful curses to the ground. In the capital city of the north – where his body hangs in the parade square, in increasingly negative metamorphosis, man made into corpse chrysalis, now a pinata for the shouting crowds – the celebrations are ugly fueled by hate. *Iggly!* they cry. *Devil!* Even a grandmother gets in on the fun, firing a pistol point-blank into his face. They showed that one on the news. There is no pity anymore. Everyone blames him for the war and the terror.

It's human nature to concentrate on the bad. I don't blame television for not knowing any better. But I knew this man as a man of great love and untroubled inner peace.

We met on the Internet, through a dating site. He sent me digital smiles. It was cute. Still, we did not click right away. I understood that dictators were difficult guys, with terrible reputations and storylines that rarely ended well. Like every girl, I just wanted something uncomplicated, to meet someone nice.

Forget about all that, this will be different, he said. In the photographs he sent me he looked like he meant it: soft blue eyes and a flat, relaxed mouth. He looked more like a man who ran a library. And yet there was something dynamic about him, too. I always thought the footage they chose for the news was entirely misleading, those jackboots and high collars. Those mirrored sunglasses didn't help either.

He explained that it was just his public persona, that it was necessary to project a certain calculated ruthlessness. *It's just the job,* he said. *You know, all that cult of personality stuff. I'm different with you. You make me different.*

He always knew what to say to me, how to shift my heart by inches. His instincts were finely attuned to soft spots and maneuver. Still, a part of me was well aware that behind the velvet charm was a necessary animal cunning.

Necessary because he had come up the hard way, through the motorcycle-pilot gangs, singing "We Will Not be Defeated" and those other drinking songs. His part in the coup had not been especially bloody but then came the purges and the *desaparecidos* and all that grim business euphemistically called *consolidation of power.* His new American friends left the usual fingerprints on the usual bags of cash. The dictator's part was mainly to stand up straight and wave his fist from the balcony. It could have been anyone in that uniform. Meanwhile, he slept with loaded pistols in both hands.

Everything was a confidence game. *If people think I am finished then I am finished,* he explained. It was difficult for me to know how much power he really had. But that voice! He persuaded me to get on a plane, to come live with him so we could start a life together. An armoured car was waiting for me at the airport.

He took me on a tour of the palace and its grounds. In the botanical gardens I held his gloved hand, squeezed his knuckles one by one.

That's Italian leather, he said. *By the way, you can never leave this place.*

That was his way of telling me that he loved me and wanted to protect me. His truth was in the details. It was what he was all about, trying to control the little things while out in the countryside the tribes were still killing each other in the wide swaths of age-old vendettas. *I just want the trains to run on time,* he said. He did his best. He was constantly working. The meetings went on night and day. There were reeducation teams, relocation teams, reallocation teams, rehabilitation teams, retaliation teams.

I believe in teamwork, he said.

Just don't try to micromanage the world, I said.

It's just a couple of lists, he said. *You can get a lot done with the right list.*

He'd wake up in the middle of the night and start scribbling in a notepad. One morning I took a look while he sang away in the shower. His handwriting was like a bed of snarled snakes.

> *Pick up ring.*
> *Ask Teresa to marry me.*
> *Buy more helicopter gunships.*

We were married at the base of a pyramid. It was a beautiful ceremony, complete with a military parade. Then came the belly dancers and the snake charmers. The American ambassador gave us a white stallion called Anti-Communist, but I changed his name to Bootsie.

We had five good years. Then terrorists blew up that airport in Los Angeles and all those judges died. When some American reporter wrote a story about how one of the terrorists had once worked for the dictator's secret police, I knew it was the beginning of the end. Democracies are big on blunt revenge.

Whereas before they only had crude sticky-bombs, now the Christian rebels had stinger missiles and proper dental care. No one talked about how dangerously socialist they were anymore. Instead the senator from New York made speeches about our country being godless.

As the security situation deteriorated so did our marriage. The firing squads kept me up at night, rattled my nerves.

We should go, I said. *We should leave this all behind.*

You cannot talk like that, he said.

So what? Now I'm not allowed to say how I feel?

I know what's best, he said.

Oh do you? Do you know what they're all saying? That dictators are bad people! That they belong in hell!

I know I am loved, he said, pulling on his bulletproof vest.

I couldn't understand what he meant at the time. The assassination attempts picked up speed. He was shot at and bombed and laced with poison. The scars on his face ran like roadways to my fear.

When the state is paranoid you live in a paranoid state. Then reality catches up to you. In the end they were all against him, it was in the graffiti all over the market, in the whispering clutches around the palace. I'd walk by and people would just stop and stare. *Iggly, Iggly man!* But the dictator didn't care.

I know I am loved, he said.

How can you say that? I'd scream.

But it was no use. He'd just smile and kiss me and say he had a phone call to make.

He always said that.

He sent me to stay in our villa in France. The next day rebels overran the palace. There are rumours that in the end he was still on the phone, smiling serenely, listening to a 1-900 number where nuns say prayers for you at $3.99 a minute, and tell you that God loves you, and all is forgiven.

Iggly! they cry. But the truth is more complicated. Truth is, we need our dictators iron-fisted, because everyone likes a winner. Just like how I, even as a young girl, always liked the cocky boys, the ones you knew were lying to you. And the people will miss their Iggly Devil soon enough as well, when the tribes have only each other to hate, and wheel of murder spins back and forth, and none of the damn trains run on time.

big head

I'm in trouble again. It's not real trouble – just Big-Head trouble, the diluted facsimile of trouble, dripping away – but like Chinese water torture the splatter tends to add up.

From: F.W.L. Dubbelman <dubbelman-fwl@vtu.ca>
Date: June 13, 2006 9:33 AM EDT (CA)
To: Sean Quintal <SeanQuintal@vtu.ca>
Subject: NON-COMPLIANCE

Mr.Quintal,
I have not seen the paperwork for your recent absence (for the date you called in sick, during the last week of May). Need I remind you that all absences from the workplace must be accompanied by the appropriate documentation, and that such documentation must be completed immediately upon your return to work.
I expect to see the forms on my desk by the end of the day.
Director of Artistic Operations,
Francis Walby Lindsey Dubbelman

Francis Walby Lindsey Dubbelman is really just Francis. Or Big Head. Francis is supervisor of the department called "Art and Design" at the Vivian Ted University for Jesus. This "department" consists of three guys: Francis, PK and me.

Francis has a big head. I don't mean just pit-bull or troglodytic big; the head that Francis sports is something wholly egregious, like some corpulent growth-hormone pumpkin. One that's rotting from the inside out. Color it all grey, add some pointy teeth, a discount haircut, two spinning-pin eyes ... it's almost a Japanese dragon, but if you try to imagine a smile then everything just seeps and sags all over the place.

So Francis is Big Head and Big Head is Francis. What else could he be? The rest of him doesn't give you anything else to work with. He's a wreck: an abused, mashed-up, ugly doll thing, falling apart at the seams, sewn back together for the purpose of scaring small children, this hideous little hobgoblin made out of stuffed balls of Kleenex.

From: F.W.L. Dubbelman <dubbelman-fwl@vtu.ca>
Date: June 13, 2006 1:11 PM EDT (CA)
To: Sean Quintal <SeanQuintal@vtu.ca>
Subject: NON-RESPONSIVE TO NON-COMPLIANCE

Mr.Quintal,
I have yet to see any response to my email of this morning.
I REPEAT:
I have not seen the paperwork for your recent absence (for the date you called in sick, during the last week in May). Need I remind you that all absences from the workplace must be accompanied by the appropriate documentation, and that such documentation must be completed IMMEDIATELY upon your return to work.
I expect to see the forms on my desk by the end of the day.
This is your second warning.
Director of Artistic Operations,
Francis Walby Lindsey Dubbelman

Now, the only part of this that really catches my attention
is how vague he is about the date. Which means that he probably doesn't have one, that he can't remember *what* day it was
that I called in sick. This is so perfectly Big Head: the blind
wind-up toy trying to be menacing, Mr. Magoo as Gauleiter.

I remember the date perfectly. It was the day that I bought
my new couch. Cool, overcast, light wind. Plump, oversized,
leather-skinned. I remember having Chinese for lunch, reading a book about Genghis Khan in a corner booth, how he
devastated the greater part of the known world, and when
he caught another king or sultan or khan he would have him
rolled up in a rug and then kicked to death, because he was
afraid of spilling royal blood on the earth. Then I went home
and had a nap. It was a very nice day.

From: Sean Quintal <SeanQuintal@vtu.ca>
Date: June 13, 2006 1:17 PM EDT (CA)
To: F.W.L. Dubbelman <dubbelman-fwl@vtu.ca>
Subject: be more specific

Francis,
What date are you talking about, exactly?
Sean

PK is reading over my shoulder, standing there spooning
mouthfuls of pie into his mouth. He doesn't even bother to
cut it up, just holds the aluminum bottom like a dinner plate
and starts shovelling. *Is Big Head on the warpath again?* he
laughs, spitting red flecks. Then he points with his spoon:
Hey, I like that. He's pointing at the other half of my screen.
It's a drawing I've done of the baptism of Jesus by John. My
John the Baptist looks bored, not nearly reverent enough, so
I'll probably have to redo the eyes.

From: F.W.L. Dubbelman <dubbelman-fwl@vtu.ca>
Date: June 13, 2006 1:21 PM EDT (CA)
To: Sean Quintal <SeanQuintal@vtu.ca>
Subject: re: be more specific

Mr.Quintal,
Date is last week in May.
D.A.O,
Francis Walby Lindsey Dubbelman

Big Head stays in his private office, bunkers himself in, only communicates with me by email. This is because every time he used to come barking I would get up and stand as close to him as possible. Big Head is five-foot-four, and most of that is head. I am six-foot-five, and heavier than I should be.

I hear better out of my right ear, I would say, very quietly, leaning in and over him.

Also: I wear cologne in layers. I wear: Hugo Boss, Alfred Sung, Calvin Klein.

Big Head is scent sensitive.

Big Head's breath is like rotting cantaloupe.

From: Sean Quintal <SeanQuintal@vtu.ca>
Date: June 13, 2006 1:42 PM EDT (CA)
To: F.W.L. Dubbelman <dubbelman-fwl@vtu.ca>
Subject: terms of reference

Francis,
Every form in every office in the world needs a date; it is one of those ubiquitous features of managerial sup-puration. The description "last week in May" is wanting. Would you give me a date, please?
Sean

PS – Maybe the form has already been processed by HR and you simply forgot about it. I should walk over there to say hi to TT anyway; do you want me to look into it?

TT is Teddy Tinlin, the president of the Vivian Ted University for Jesus. Teddy and his late-wife Vivian ran a nationwide chain of shoe stores before cashing it all in to pursue their real passion for educating today's youth in the loving ways of Jesus Christ. TT is tanned and relaxed, has had some exposure to advertising and likes the way I draw.

TT is always sending me congratulatory emails spilling over with exclamation marks for some poster or brochure or book cover I did. Which is better than any union, better than being somebody's cousin.

From: F.W.L. Dubbelman <dubbelman-fwl@vtu.ca>
Date: June 13, 2006 2:32 PM EDT (CA)
To: Sean Quintal <SeanQuintal@vtu.ca>
Subject: NON-COMPLIANCE

Mr.Quintal,
I have several voicemails into HR even as I type this.
All absences from your work station must be approved by me in advance. Since we are on the subject of hours of work, it has been brought to my attention by several high-placed sources that there is an ongoing problem with your punctuality with regards to hours of operation, which, as you are well aware, are 0900 to 1700 hrs. Breaks (two) are fifteen minutes. Lunch is 0.5 hrs.
Any deviation from the above specified program must be approved by me in advance, preferably in writing!
Director of Artistic Operations at
Vivian Ted University for Jesus,
Francis Walby Lindsey Dubbelman

I draw Jesus fasting in the desert. I draw Jesus tempted three times by the devil. I draw Jesus preaching to the Samaritans. I draw Jesus smiling beatifically at wide-eyed African children. I draw Jesus shaking hands with businessmen, seeking corporate sponsorship.

PK's style is more conducive to a conservative, traditional Jesus, while I draw freaky Jesus, the radical and hellraiser who kicked the moneylenders out of the temple. PK draws for parents and donors. I get to be more illustrative and figurative – the graphic-novel Jesus for the kids. It's a bit much, this constant drawing and redrawing of the world's most famous carpenter, but it's too late for me, I'm lumbered with my craft.

I draw and I draw; the lines wander into my sleep. I draw him until his hair curls malevolently, until his beard flicks out in flame.

Meanwhile, Big Head walks around with his pants pulled up into the crack of his ass.

From: Sean Quintal <SeanQuintal@vtu.ca>
Date: June 13, 2006 2:50 PM EDT (CA)
To: F.W.L. Dubbelman <dubbelman-fwl@vtu.ca>
Subject: still not being very specific

Francis,
Which "high-placed sources" are you talking about?
And what, exactly, were their complaints?
Sean

Big Head couldn't draw a stick figure in a game of hangman. All he can do is photo-manipulate things on his computer. Trouble is, there's not a lot of photographs of Jesus kicking around. So PK and I draw Jesus doing what we need him to do, in all his holy contortions, while Big Head deals with the generic stuff, photographs of buildings and crosses and peaceful-looking trees for the backgrounds of the brochures by the front door that no one cares about.

PK stands at the window, eating his pie, checking out whatever female student saunters by on the sidewalk below. He lifts his leg to fart. His t-shirt says: *You run an engine this hot, you're gonna spill a little gas.* He wears that thing all the time.

From: F.W.L. Dubbelman <dubbelman-fwl@vtu.ca>
Date: June 13, 2006 3:43 PM EDT (CA)
To: Sean Quintal <SeanQuintal@vtu.ca>
Subject: NON-COMPLIANCE

Mr.Quintal,
There are also ongoing problems with: low-productivity, a relaxed attitude towards deadlines, the inefficient use of downtime, and the incorrect completion of Progress Reports.
Low Productivity. Example: The quality of your recent poster for the "Jesus is Here, Jesus is Now" midnight prayer vigil did not correspond to the length of time you took to complete it.
Deadlines: Clients around the campus need to have confidence in our ability to handle short turnaround times, especially when promoting the "Spontaneous Grace" events.
Use of Time: All downtime should be used for training. I have provided several instructional videos on the Adobe Photoship filter effects, all of which have remained unopened in our resource center.
Project Reports: Your processing of these is non-compliant. I have stated repeatedly that I want these submitted to me in the following format:
Client
Date Received
Date Due
Percentage of completion timing as of today
Estimated timing to completion

DAO at VTUJ,
Francis Walby Lindsey Dubbelman

Big Head loves the filters in Photoshop. He is constantly embossing things, blurring things, creating false shadows, putting people's distorted heads in crystal balls.

Some of the old guys around here actually love it, too. They think he's a genius. *Look!* Big Head says to some hapless "professor." *Look at this picture! What do you see in the last window on the top floor? Yes sir, that's my face! I always sneak one in!*

Big Head drives a little purple sportscar. Convertible. Seeing him in it reminds me of these toys I had when I was a kid, I think they were called PipSqueaks. You hit their heads and they squeaked.

From: Sean Quintal <SeanQuintal@vtu.ca>
Date: June 13, 2006 4:10 PM EDT (CA)
To: F.W.L. Dubbelman <dubbelman-fwl@vtu.ca>
Subject: non-compliance

Francis,
a) You still haven't told me the source or exact nature of these "complaints."
b) The "Jesus is Here, Jesus is Now" poster took longer than expected because the client kept changing her mind as to what she wanted Jesus to be wearing. The "Jesus is Now" aspect – Jesus in a blue suit and Oxford tie – just made him look like an upscale drug dealer. I did try to warn her. As it was I had to redraw him from scratch (as per your recent instructions against "recycling" artwork). Perhaps you have some original Jesus artwork that we could bank for the future?
c) I very much doubt if my "turnaround" time will ever be fast enough for the Spontaneous Grace events, considering their spontaneity.
d) I already know enough about Photoshop, thanks. (By

"resource center," do you mean that pile of junk on top of the filing cabinet by the door?)

e) Your format for Progress Reports makes no sense. I hardly know the "Percentage of completion timing as of today" [sic] until I've gone through all the revisions, and I hardly know how many revisions there's going to be ahead of time. Same goes for "Esitmated timing to completion" [sic].

Besides, what's the point of all this anyway?

Sean

PS – Locate that form yet?

Big Head doesn't smoke, drink or do drugs.

Big Head doesn't exercise or read or watch birds.

Big Head has a picture of himself wearing a tuxedo on his personal website.

Big Head has tea every day at ten o'clock with a woman who wears a full beard. He takes her into his office and shuts the door. I heard she used to be a missionary in China, pre-beard days, until I guess even the Chinese grew afraid.

Big Head reads computer manuals and *The Power of Thinking Really Big* and the Bible.

Big Head compiles files. On me. I hope he eventually gets it all bound in quality leatherette hard cover, so he has something to reminisce with in retirement.

PK's second favourite t-shirt says: *I can't believe how much heat this thing generates.*

From: F.W.L. Dubbelman <dubbelman-fwl@vtu.ca>
Date: June 13, 2006 4:19 PM EDT (CA)
To: Sean Quintal <SeanQuintal@vtu.ca>
Subject: MORE NON-COMPLIANCE

Mr.Quintal,
Other non-compliance issues:
1) The notice you provide when going to medical appointments is insufficient. Staffing and coverage issues are not adequately considered.
2) Time spent on email, Internet and phone is excessive. Phone is for porfessional use only.
3) Jurnalling is not part of yor job description. Writing in jornal should be allookated to brakes and lunch.
4) Excessave colone use is a form of assault. Workplace health and safety issues states no use of sense.
5) Beards and sandals are not apporpriate or professional dress for an institution of higher learnding.
DAO at Vivian Ted University for Jesus,
Francis Walby Lindsey Dubbelman

Big Head waltzes in wearing a flourescent pink baseball cap. It sits like an upside-down teacup on the top of his head.

Big Head waltzes in wearing some kind of carpal-tunnel brace, his arm all twisted around, his face buckled in for extra sympathy.

Big Head waltzes in at ten o'clock in the morning, just in time for his closed-door circus break with the Bearded Lady.

Big Head goes to the other side of the campus to use the washroom.

Big Head waltzes out to the parking lot at two o'clock in the afternoon, an empty folder under one arm.

Big Head disappears for most of the day, then waltzes in at 4:30, just to make sure I stick around until 5:00. This is one of his more sporting moods, when he wears a sweater draped over his shoulders and tied in front, like some outrageously queened-up tennis pro.

When he *is* here, Big Head spends most of his time on his freelance cash cow, *The Journal of Midwestern Prisons*. It is desktop publishing at its most banal, a magazine with all the turgid, condemned grace of a piss-stained photograph of Queen Victoria.

Big Head doesn't worry about getting caught because he is superior, better than everyone else, *they're just jealous*.

Big Head whistles and hums, tries to keep his shoulders straight, tries to look bigger than he is, but if you meet him in the hall, he'll avoid eye contact. His safari shorts have a pressed crease, his black socks are pulled up to the knee. His face is shiny.

Big Head looks the way Charlie Brown would look if Lucy tortured him for a few years in a concentration camp, then tried to fatten him up at the last minute.

> From: Sean Quintal <SeanQuintal@vtu.ca>
> Date: June 13, 2006 4:20 PM EDT (CA)
> To: F.W.L. Dubbelman <dubbelman-fwl@vtu.ca>
> Subject: re: non-compliance
>
> Francis,
> So ... you still haven't found that form then.
> Sean

Maybe this was revenge. Maybe this was for all the times the other kids pushed him into the snowbank, for every jock who clotheslined him, swept him spinning off his feet, just because that big, bulbous head was such a juicy target.

I'll show you! Big Head must have said. *I may be small but I'm mighty!*

I can tell by the growing rate of spelling mistakes that he's exhausted now, slouched over in his jacked-up chair, that little paunch creased in tight against his rib cage, panting away. Someday it might all be worth it, someday Teddy Tinlin will die and then Big Head will have his sweet sweet revenge, that well-practiced firing speech delivered at the most delicious frequency, every vowel and consonant a delectation, like purple flowers spilling from his mouth. What a speech, what a speech it will be ...

> From: F.W.L. Dubbelman <dubbelman-fwl@vtu.ca>
> Date: June 13, 2006 4:33 PM EDT (CA)
> To: Sean Quintal <SeanQuintal@vtu.ca>
> Subject: NO RECORD OF YOUR COMPLIANCE
>
> Mr.Quintal,
> HR has just infromed me that there is no records of you compleetioning the apporpriate paperwork for your absensse during the last wek in May.
> I expects some form of satisfactorys resolution to this by the end of the day.
> Also: I have not reciieved your request for your holiday leaves yet. With your present workload September would be the best time for absance. Please remember that annual absanse is to be approved in advanceds of the dates requesteds.
> Director of Artistic Operations at
> Vivian Ted University for Jesus,
> Francis Walby Lindsey Dubbelman

Somewhere in that misshapen skull of his, in some low-trajectory orbit around the greasy sun of his consciousness, I know that Big Head wants to think of himself as some kind of artist, wants people to see him as dynamic, as creative, as something special. If only he could admit that he is a fraud, that his only talents lie in dissembling and hackery, in being a tricksy, vulgar, unaccountable sham-artist, then I would have all the respect in the world for him. And I wouldn't have these stray daydreams about walking into his office with a hammer and nails.

> From: Sean Quintal <SeanQuintal@vtu.ca>
> Date: June 13, 2006 4:44 PM EDT (CA)
> To: Ted Tinlin <TedTinlin@vtu.ca>

Subject: holidays

Ted,
How are things? It's a bit slow over here in the art department; you should drop by for a visit when you have a chance. I'm thinking of taking some holidays in the middle of July, maybe go on a trip, try to enjoy the summer. How about you?
Cheers,
Sean

I draw the Sermon on the Mount. I draw Jesus on the Road to Damascus. I draw Thomas and his doubting finger, poking around.

Big Head waltzes by with a haircut that looks like the aftermath of a cruel party game, like someone came running at him with a pair of clippers and half missed.

Best six dollars I ever spent, says PK, in his nasal, imitation-Big-Head voice. *Hey, come here, you gotta check this out.* He's always calling me over to his computer, always it's another home video of some German Shepherd or Belgian or Bernese Mountain Dog doing some kind of trick, jumping on a trampoline or using a knife and fork or playing the fucking piano.

That's cute, I say, standing there just long enough so I can walk away.

From: Ted Tinlin <TedTinlin@vtu.ca>
Date: June 26, 2006 4:50 PM EDT (CA)
To: Sean Quintal <SeanQuintal@vtu.ca>
Subject: re: holidays

Hey there Sean!
Always good to hear from you!
By the way, great work on that "Continue to Walk with Jesus" mailer! We're getting a super response!
Enjoy your holidays in July!

He is Risen!
Teddy Tinlin

When I was a kid I went to Sunday School. Most kids did. You didn't have to be particularly religious; I can't remember my mom going to church at all, although she made *us* go all the time. I would usually pray for Jesus to let me escape some bad behaviour I'd recently committed, like stealing cartons of cigarettes out of trucks or porno mags from the back of the Chinese restaurant or setting fire to some abandoned house. Sometimes it even worked.

My nephews don't go to Sunday School. They wouldn't know Jesus if he climbed down off the cross and handed them a Playstation. Their favorite story is the Gingerbread Man.

> *Run, run, as fast as you can,*
> *You can't catch me*
> *I'm the Gingerbread Man!*

They're nearly obsessed with the perfect ending: a tragic hubris that culminates with the hop-skip-two-step of death. For them, the Gingerbread Man's arrogant sing-song makes the wolf's cunning *coup de maître* all that more delicious.

That's too bad, I say. *All he wanted was to be left alone.*

Yeah, but he didn't have to be such a jerk about it! says Cody, the older of the two.

Yeah, too bad! says Callum, not really knowing who he's agreeing with.

From: Sean Quintal <SeanQuintal@vtu.ca>
Date: June 26, 2006 4:57 PM EDT (CA)
To: F.W.L. Dubbelman <dubbelman-fwl@vtu.ca>
Subject: paperwork

Francis,
The paperwork you want is in your letter slot. I

randomly chose the 30th of May. That's a Tuesday.
There's also a form for some holidays I'm taking in
July. 12th to the 19th. I've already run this by Ted.
Cheers,
Sean

Jonny Magnum had no hands. Instead he had guns where his hands should have been. It was a violent way to live.

It wasn't always this way. For most of his life Jonny had large but fluid hands, they moved over things so easily, and with those hands he made robots. He made robots with hydraulics and circuit boards and keypads, little three-foot-tall robots, single-purpose thinking machines that would mow the lawn on Sundays or serve drinks from the basement bar or always remember to feed the fish, and never overfeed them. Jonny wasn't practical like a mechanic or serious like a scientist or even neat and meticulous like an anesthesiologist but he did try to create things that would fix or improve or add charm where before there was only a need and an absence, something missing but imminent like the smell of approaching rain. He always wanted people to give their robots names just as they would a hamster or a snake, those things that have life but are limited or contained. He thought of it as animation in context. He ran low-budget ads on Saturday-morning television, the kind where the guy holds up handmade signs, the kind that change every week, and at the end of each one he'd say, *If I can't build you a robot that makes you smile, then I will smash that robot and give you your money back with my own flesh and blood hands.* People would ask him *How can you afford to do that?* and he'd always reply, *Hey, no one wants to see a robot die, you just have to have a little faith.*

Jonny's own favourite robot was named Simon. Simon could sort screws (Jonny hated sorting screws) while singing the soundtrack to *Grease*. And at the end of the last song he would laugh a little shower of sparks and say *thank you, thank you* and then go back to sleep.

One morning, dropping sugar cubes into his too-strong coffee, standing there in the carpeted hallway of a hotel, Jonny Magnum found love at a gun show. He wasn't even supposed to be there; he was supposed to be at the amateur robotics convention on the next floor. But when he walked by the gun show he saw the coffee in the hallway and and then he saw her, this woman, just inside the convention hall, sliding along like a three-second movie, perfectly framed by the open double doors. He saw blonde hair in half curls, a thin neck and the line of her jaw curving to the set of her mouth in a little smile. He saw nice white thighs in that perfect thickness that only women can have, the kind a man sees and then unconsciously grinds his teeth. Jonny stopped, stepped backwards, poked his head inside. The place was alive with men, short and quick like insects at work, moving from booth to booth to point at guns, reach for guns, touch as many guns as they could, while no one was touching or watching this woman at all. And for Jonny that was enough of a damn shame to make him go in and stand right beside her.

Isn't this nice? she said, pointing out a Beretta Cougar semi-automatic in hard chrome.

It certainly is, Jonny said.

They talked for a few minutes about guns, mostly Jonny was just nodding his head. Then she turned to him and smiled.

My name's Charlotte, she said.

Charlotte, Jonny repeated. *Say Charlotte, why don't I come over to your house and take a bath, and you could sit on the edge of the tub and show me your favourite pair of shoes?*

Charlotte laughed, that wide-eyed way that girls do when you catch them in the schoolyard. *Oh my God, aren't you a flirty one!*

Look, Jonny said, leaning in close to her neck. *I'm not dangerous but I'm not exactly handicapped either, if you know what I mean, and somewhere in between is the idea that I would never forgive myself if I said anything less than the truth to you.*

Charlotte moved her eyes to look into his but did not pull away. *Doesn't matter at all*, she said. *I'm not from around here anyway.*

Jonny stayed still. *Uh mmmm.*

But I do have a room in this hotel, she said. *A room with a hot tub.*

She did not have her favourite pair of shoes with her, of course, but she did have her *least* favourite pair – *Oh my God, aren't these ugly?* she cried – and between the hot tub and a nearby shooting range they had the kind of surprising weekend that make people promise things quickly. *I want to move here*, Charlotte whispered, *to be with you, you'll just have to give me a few months to sort some things out.*

Together they moved to the next stage, this love affair in letters and phone calls and plans *down the road*. Jonny did his best. He wrote carefully. He looked up words for her. He bought a bigger house for her. He built special robots for her. Gun robots. He taught Simon to sing her favourite song. And when she came to visit, she would lie quietly on his bed and let him put his hands all over her. *You have lovely grooves*, Jonny said, hearing the blood in his ears.

In the next stage the spaces between visits became longer and longer. Anxiety moved in. It was not Jonny's nature to press or push but after two years he could hardly stand it, all the parts were ready and he just wanted to build a life with her – until that started it felt like the world was holding its breath. Finally, one night on the phone, the question spilled out of him: *When are you moving, Charlotte? When are you coming to be with me?*

I don't know, Charlotte said.

Charlotte, I need to know.

And then Charlotte, in gasps like a moaning engine, started crying.

Jonny stood still in the middle of his living room. He listened to her breathing, wet and close, this storm in his ear, and in his mind it was like the scattering of a cloud of birds, the sensation of a thousand cold shadows. Then he took the phone down to his workshop, placed it on the table, face-up so she could hear him, and started assembling his tools. In the background, Simon was singing.

on the day of
your release

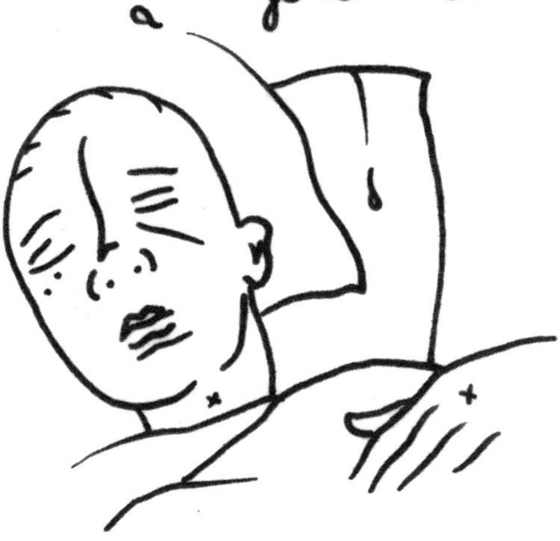

On the day of your release (Form 121-A, *not* pink) the quality of sleep is kinetic, that soft-drum transit state like hypnosis, seamlessly smooth and automatic, thrumming alive and arriving in anticipation of the alarm and what lies beyond it. Wake ... up. This is *Good Morning*, that good-good morning that patters in all of us like a child's bare feet in the kitchen or the hallway or somewhere else you might find that slap-slap sound, maybe the cement skirt of a public pool. The important thing is to understand that the time is *now* and it might as well be Christmas, everything's so electric that all you can be is elastic and happy inside.

Get up. Get up on your feet, throw open the curtains, close your eyes and stand naked tip-toe before the sun and s-t-r-e-t-c-h. Beneath your eyelids is the old biorhythmic light-show, pulsing flares with wavering tails, a half-lit private universe that you can squeeze to make the stars explode. It's pretty cool. What's also cool is that you have a huge erection bobbing around.

The radio alarm lurches to life but it's just right, not too loud, actually quite pleasant and guess what? The forecast is good. Keep stretching. Make your fingers touch the ceiling, twist from side to side. These are easy, efficient movements where randomly oppressive elements like constricted spines or restricted chests or thoughtless handfuls of hair-failure are not even things remembered, let alone weighed or grieved. Instead: CALM. There is time to stand there, composed and breathing, enjoying the mere phenomenon of your extant being. *Nothing but clear skies ahead*, the weatherman says.

You go about your morning rituals in perfect leisure: a hot shower for open pores, a razor that cuts clean, easily managed hair and good coffee and deliberate minutes for a newspaper over breakfast. Your favourite team won the Stanley Cup months ago but the sports section runs a follow-up story anyway, just to revel in it. Where are your keys? Right where they should be, on the telephone table by the door. How ridiculous is the hall mirror now, when you already know how good you look?

You do the drive to work in record time: lanes empty, every light flashing yellow. There are no noises of metal on metal, no failure of electricity on the passenger-side window, no random rattlings of frame or mind. Your car hums. In fact, you can barely feel it beneath you, around you, there is only that plush notion of safety and reassurance. You roll down the windows and let the world come through. It is one of those mornings that make you think about seeing, the scenery streaked like remastered film, soaked with colour and sunshine, searing itself into you, vivid and beautiful. That dark-blonde woman who is always walking her dog waves as you wash by. You pretend not to see her.

First one at the office. You pull into Sack Face's spot and remove the little metal plate that says "Reserved / Director." Of course you have a screwdriver; there's a full tool kit in your trunk today.

You also have keys to the building, one of the few entrusted, so once inside you renew the faith for one last time, flicking the place into life: row after row of fluorescent lights, then the colour printer, then the copier. Then you make coffee. It's three scoops today, fuck two.

Needing a box to pack up the personal effects from your desk, you go looking in the warehouse. There's a small pyramid of computers back there, last year's model, barely used, they're upgrading again, pointlessly, this lot being shunted off to the nether regions of a failing corporate empire. You take one out to the trunk of your car.

People start coming in, wandering really, looking small and shaken. Your eyes run over them without a single consideration as to the utility of blunt implements (stapler, phone, can of Zoodles from bottom drawer, etc) for reducing certain individuals to broken clots of flesh. They've lost that power now and you feel only a diffused sense of sympathy for them, like for the old guys who beg in front of the liquor store or the sleeping figures in a Henry Moore drawing or polar bears pacing a cage in the summertime or some other creatures that are hopeless or otherwise diminished by their circumstances.

Your co-workers form a respectful queue to say their goodbyes, all confusion and grief and shabby clothes, coffee mugs held reverently before them, saying how sorry they are to see you go, *How sad it is, how sad*. You do your best to console them, *Come on now, you'll be fine*, but they can no longer hear, just nodding and looking away and then going on to comment on how damn good the coffee is for once, *boy it's really fucking good*.

On the day of your release there is yet another meeting of the Rationalization Committee that you don't need to go to but you can't help yourself, you're drawn to the idea of croissants on square blue napkins and sure enough the entire exercise is just a platform for the little private-school prick called Hamilton-Paterson to give a long, facile lecture on professionalism. At the end of it he asks for any questions. *Just one*, you say, finger raised, standing up for effect. *You know what that speech was like? That was like watching a little pig get up on its hind legs and talk about table manners*. People are still laughing as you goose-step out, giving Hamilton-Paterson the shoulder as you go by.

Back at your desk there is a note from Svetlana ... Svetlana the receptionist, Svetlana from the front desk and this is a thing meant more for pulp paper, like the cover of some cheap paperback showing a woman spilling out of her red dress, black eyes and parted lips and big creamy breasts, under a title like *Wanton Lust* or *Flesh Fiesta* or *Wanton Fiesta Flesh Lust*. Anyway this is what comes to mind while sitting there holding this scrap of paper: *I want to buy you lunch* it reads, the letters like little snakes, looping and writhing on a white sea. Also, the word *want* is underlined at least three or four times.

On the day of your release the pleasure of this moment is interrupted by a shadow, by a greasy queasiness in the form of Sack Face standing there in the doorway of your cubicle, grotesque and beckoning. *Time for the exit interview*, he says, and your bowels clench.

On the day of your release Sack Face is whistling on the way to his office, a little man's bravado, trying to conjure the layers of will necessary to ward off certain facts which only now are swarming over him. You look at the clustered tubes along the curve of his spine at the back of his neck. And smile.

On the day of your release it all comes down to you and Sack Face, and he can only keep it together for a little while, jumpy voiced, his porcelain coffee cup rattling in his hand, on the saucer, halfway through the thick file he completely loses it, breaking down into a wet slab of something less than human, that horrible paper-bag face held like despair in his hands, going on and on about how this is all his fault, it's his failure, *Just like everything, I'm a fraud a fake a pathetic forgery* he moans but already you're getting bored with this shit so out comes the flame-thrower and that old skin like tissue sure burns bright and blue, you're standing there screaming righteousness like Genghis Khan: *IF YOU HAD NOT COMMITTED GREAT SINS, GOD WOULD NOT HAVE SENT A PUNISHMENT LIKE ME UPON YOU*, and sure enough Sack Face morphs into this giant, squealing rat, certainly it must be destroyed, the entire office is crowded at the doorway applauding, Svetlana right at the front, licking her lips and smiling like sex in an alley, and amidst all this you can feel that special ethereal hand on your shoulder, it might be Jesus or Buddha or one of those aliens with the special sneakers, whoever it is says *You've done some nice work here today* and *make sure you check those lottery tickets on the way home.*

Don't let anyone tell you that you don't deserve this.

On the day of your release you never set the alarm in the first place, not wanting to lose the dream, sleeping through the morning with its blunt rain against the window, and then all afternoon as well, missing the whole thing. Then the phone rings.

locomotive

Nathan walked home. *I am walking home.* He was bent into it.

He wondered how he looked, about the angle of his determination. *I'm sure I look fine. Besides, the street is empty.* But there was a quiver, an urge in him to glance backwards, to look for telling droplets in the snow.

What am I? He often thought this, when diminished. *I am head-down deliberate, concentrating on the sidewalk here, where it should be, beneath this crooked path of packed snow. I am thoughtful enough to see these footprints as interesting – look at the way they cluster and converge, there's a rhythm involved in following them, you have to try to match the strides of the previous pedestrians, who in their turn have all tried to match each other. You have to be careful, you have to pick your way along. If you choose the errant footprints, the ones to the side, you will find them to be frozen hard, like ice, and problematic if they are too small, because surely they will twist you down. Surely.* Nathan tried to put his foot in a spot that was too small. *Yes, this is a problem.* Then he fell.

Nathan was lying in someone's yard, on a mound of snow that had been shovelled from the front walk. It had a crisp top layer that cracked like eggshell around him. Slowly he rolled over on his back so that he could look from side to side. There was no one to see. *This is quite comfortable. I might stay here awhile.* The wind moaned in the treetops above him.

With one gloved hand he pulled his overcoat tight, covering his legs. He kept the other hand tucked beneath, squeezed to his ribs. The distress in his side was undeniable. The pain had a piercing quality about it – that was no surprise – but it was more about something being wrong within him, something defiled, spoiled and spreading. *A knife is such a low-technology instrument, so treacherous and personal, so antimodern. One thinks of Caligula or Caesar. In our own century it is entirely a surprise.* In fact, the only example which came to mind was the black-and-white photograph of the stricken Japanese socialist Inejiro Asanuma, murdered on black-and-white television, his screaming assassin theatrically pulling back the bloodied blade with both hands, while Asanuma looked curdled, ruined, his glasses tumbling. *I hope I didn't make a face like that,* Nathan whispered out loud. Asanuma's nickname was "The Human Locomotive," one of those peculiar Japan-isms meant to express unstoppable force and energy. *Time to get up,* Nathan announced.

He rolled himself over to his knees. With his one free hand he scooped snow over the red blotch where he had lain. In a swoon, seeing stars, he pushed upwards, his face to the sky, then steadied himself and got back on the path.

What am I? I am a man just trying to get home. And if I can just get home then everything will be fine. Really, how deep could she have pushed the thing? He wiped some bubbles from the corner of his mouth, took a wet breath, and started moving.

Look at this – this first day of spring and winter still has its claws, the wind is picking up, tearing around with stinging bits of ice, roaring in my ears, polishing the streets to gleaming, and the trees wave their hands in wicked benediction, and the grim rows of hedges grab at me as I pass, and I have to remember that it's just a late afternoon in March in Winnipeg, and not some scene from Brueghel, with its colours of catastrophe, its seeping browns and blotted blacks and muted blue-grays against his heartless backdrops of white, and I have to walk straighter with these people around now, these stark figures hurrying along, like sticks rolling over ice, their movements crisp then blurring at the edges, coal to slate to silver, it really is quite beautiful, and I hope to God I'm not dying.

What am I? he whispered. *I am not dying. I have my hopes. And breathing is so important.*

On the last hundred yards up the hill to his house Nathan passed a pair of staring children, bleary like vapour, who filled him with sudden shame. In his doorway he balanced himself against the frame, struggling with keys that were slick with blood. *How lucky that is*, he said, when he saw the open notepad and pen already there on the kitchen table. And sitting down ... *Well, it's like heaven*. Leaning in on both elbows, he wrote:

> Deandra,
> How graceless. You might as well have spit on me
> from a moving train, stuck your head out the win-
> dow to laugh at my tacky flowers as you pulled
> away.
> Nathan
>
> P.S. I may be, as you say, ridiculous, but you, my
> dear, are clearly mad. And although I promised
> never to mention it, I think we were both better off
> in that Other Place, and I think you should go back
> there, as soon as you can.

Nathan wanted to write more but his thoughts were thinning out now, his breathing shallow. He could hear the sound of dripping but when he looked up at that space below the tap there was nothing there. He remembered the time he dyed Deandra's hair at the kitchen sink, the invitation that was the nape of her neck, how lovely and serene she looked with her eyes closed to the warm running water, her lopsided smile at the crinkly feel of plastic gloves, the shiny red drops on his kitchen floor. He put his head down on the table to stare at them for a little while longer. Then he would get up, he promised.

simone calling

Simone likes to call me at three or four in the morning. She likes to get a few drinks in before sending that electronic ring-pulse trawling through my head. Of course at first I can't make sense of it, staggering blind out to the living room to be confronted by her plastic echo on the answering machine, that red light signalling life in the darkness. *Come on Quintal, get up, I know you're there, answer the fucking phone, I'm just going to keep calling so you might as well answer.* A pulsing beep cuts her off but a few seconds later the phone starts ringing again, it's loud and slapping at the top of my head so stooping to disconnect the chord from the jack is automatic, I make that little noise like I've spilled something and then stumble back to bed. My good friend Simone: she will do this four or five times a month before she forgets me for six.

It's late September when I'm travelling to her city to see other people. I tell Simone by email.

Simone: *So you're going to stay at my house, right?*

Me: *Sorry honey, I've already made other arrangements. Besides, you live way out at the south end of the city and I won't have a car. I have a lot of people to see. Why don't we just meet for dinner one night?*

Simone: *Hey, why don't you quit being such a bastard and just give me some quality time for a change? We'll have a barbecue at my place and you can stay over and the next morning when I go to work I'll drop you off downtown so you can run back to your little chum-bums. Okay?*

Me: *That sounds great. I think.*

Simone: *Shut up.*

We agree on a Sunday and I spend that afternoon at a friend's house waiting for her. She's supposed to pick me up at five but she keeps calling every half hour to give me updates on why it's going to be sooner but later at the same time. I finally get into her car around eight. It's the Simone I remember, that familiar second of being shocked at how female she is in person, only now a little older, more hair and darker and more push-up to her bra. Her four-year-old frowns at me from the back seat but I give her a skipping rope with wooden handles made to look like frogs, ten minutes later she gets a grilled-cheese sandwich from the drive-thru so she's all blonde smiles until we get home.

We're in the front door for maybe a minute before the teeth-brushing argument begins. On my way out to the back deck I see the kitchen is a disaster of piles and stacks. Simone appears at the patio doors long enough to push a beer into my hand, says *Just stay here while I put Plasma to bed.*

I steal a cigarette from an open pack on the picnic table, sit down and look around the yard. The grass is patchy, the tool shed has a tilt, and the plastic toys scattered around have that bleached look from garage sales and the sun. Also: it's nine o'clock at night and I'm starving.

Hey Quintal, you kind of look like a loser sitting there by yourself, Simone says. She has her own beer and is lighting a cigarette and I know I won't be eating for a while.

When you finish that smoke we should go do those dishes, I say.

Fuck Quintal, I've been running around all day. Can we just sit here for a few minutes?

Yeah okay, sorry. So tell me how you've been.

Okay, I guess. Actually that's a lie. Actually I'm pretty lonely. It's nice to have some adult company.

You should have told me this was going to be an adult-rated evening, I say, flaring my nostrils.

Shut up. To tell you the truth I don't even think about that anymore. All the guys I meet are fucking losers. I met this one guy, a lawyer, a bit of a momma's boy, he still lived at home but he seemed okay, we went out for dinner and it was nice, we had an okay time, and at the end of it he says, I'd like to see you again but I have to leave town for a few weeks, why don't I fly you and Plasma out to Vancouver and I'll put you up in a suite. And I'm like, What the fuck? And he says, Well, I just thought you could make a little holiday out of it, no strings attached.

Sounds great, I say. *I don't what your problem is.*

Yeah, you're right, that sounds excellent, I'll just use all my vacation time for a guy I've had one dinner with, or maybe I'll just quit my job altogether, plus I'm sure this guy will be happy to shell out a couple grand just to see me and Plasma have a vacation, I'm sure he won't be expecting anything at all. But I just said, Oh yeah, I'll have to think about it, and then I didn't return his calls. So then a couple a days later he sends me this email, Hey bitch, I don't know what your problem is, I was just trying to do you a favour. Yeah whatever, fuck you buddy.

I'm laughing. *That's such a beautiful story, Simone.*

Isn't it? It really warms me up inside.

*Hey, we're not all like that. There's still a couple of nice ones
floating around.*

*I know. I just have to be extra careful because of Plasma. We
went through enough with Travis.*

*Hey, do you want me to start the barbecue so it warms up
while we do the dishes?*

*Fuck Quintal, I'm not going to beg you to be my friend, just
sit there and talk to me for a minute. Do you want another
beer?*

No, I'm good right now. Actually it's a little cool out here.

*Oh, it's a little cold. Hey, do you want to borrow some of my
panties? Fuck Quintal, this soooo reminds me of college, you
always had a thousand excuses not to have a good time.*

*Yeah, I remember a lot of those good times ... us ending up at
some party at four o'clock in the morning with no ride and no
money and you completely trashed, five guys looking at you
like breakfast and me trying to figure out how to get us out of
there in one piece.*

Simone is grinning through smoke. *Hey, what can I say,
that's what friends are for.*

*Yeah, you totally had me covered. I appreciate that. Speak-
ing of bad ideas, how's your brother these days?*

*He's nuts. He thinks there's ghosts in his house and he sleeps
with a loaded gun.*

So, he's doing better then?

Exactly. Simone points at my shorts. *So uh, are you going to tell me what's in your pocket or what?*

Oh, it's just this little book I picked up for the plane. It's about the conquistadors.

Oh yeah, where's that?

It's not a where, it's a who. They were these overrighteous Spanish guys who plundered Central and South America. Old World versus New World.

That's cool. I have a book about Native American legends. Want me to read you some?

How about after the dishes?

How about you shut the fuck up and just sit there and listen?

Simone's favourite stories are about what I'd expect, this or that animal teaching a lesson or playing a trick or otherwise coming to embody some natural element. And then some entity called Esaugetuh Emissee put it all together, I guess. It's completely dark when Simone shuts the book. I'm hunched and freezing. *You're kind of bored by this, eh?* Simone says. *Okay fuck, let's go do those dishes.*

Simone puts the pork in the oven instead of the barbecue, and while she washes and I dry, the kitchen warms up. Looking in the fridge for something to throw together for Plasma's lunch the next day, Simone comes across some leftover pizza which I eat immediately. By the time the pork tenderloin is ready I'm starting to feel capable again.

Fuck Quintal, you must have been hungry.

A few hours later she's in the middle of some story about what an asshole her boss is when the bottom suddenly gives out, she just stops and sags and says *Fuck Quintal if I don't go to bed right now I'm gonna die.* We all sleep downstairs on fold-out couches, *It's too hot and stuffy up there* Simone says. She brings Plasma down to sleep with her. My own couch is long enough even if the blanket isn't, I'm looking at my toes in the half-light when I feel Simone's hair on my face, she's leaning over me and squeezing my arm and kissing me on the cheek and for that moment I'm full and warm and thinking about old worlds. But only for a moment.

Hating her creator and life as a carnival stripper, Beulah took a rope down to the docks. The river was all gone now.

Long way down. Why can't a person touch bottom, bounce back up and start over? Even just to work with lepers. Used slow, like uncoiling rope, a rope no longer than thought.

Polly Jean. Miss Polly Jean. That was in the early eighties. Don't ask me to name the year, I've already explained all that. But yes, I do remember her. You don't forget the ones you don't forget. I mean, like the memorable ones, you know? I have her voice, right here with the others.

She's a little charmer, let me tell you, always trying to get more attention than the rest. She does have a special place in my heart, that's for sure. Maybe because she was the youngest. I do like her story so very much. And she tells it so well: that singsong in her voice, that crazy way she looked at things.

Anyway, this is her story ...

Another Friday morning in another strange place. Hullo Alberta, hullo Saskatchewan, hullo Manitoba, hullo Saskatchewan again. This was Polly Jean, thinking in nods, the provinces arrayed in atlas yellow, pink, and brown as she zigzagged along, linking towns with blinking bulbs in her mind. These were weak and lonely spots, hard to find on maps because of their tiny writing, *onetwothreefourfivesixseven* and there you go, her whole life traced out like the trajectory of a wonky rocket.

Except nothing was so robotic or planned out. These places were more like living things, like animals, thrashing around, and for the first few days somewhere new Polly Jean would always have a look at the thing, see if it had legs, see if it would stand up. Playing *THE PREDICTION GAME*, spotting omens in colourations: for example, a red bank was always a good sign, while a grey hotel was not. I am seeing the signs of the beast, she always thought, trying to be spooky with something she heard in church once. And then she had read about the Romans and their animal entrails, about looking for the future in guts. And she was just as serious about her own game, in fact almost hard and sick inside, tempered and afraid and with an eye to appeal, Umm, hulloo up there, it's Polly Jean, because it was not so much fun when the beast turned out bad, its wet eyes staring right back through you, and everything was going south again. What could you do to save yourself? I have to break the back of this thing, she'd say, I have to break the back of this thing before it walks right over me.

It was her uncle's expression: her favourite uncle, Uncle Jack, so she never called him One-Eyed Jack like everyone else. He was only one-eyed because of some place in Korea called Kapyong where a whole Chinese army tried to charge up his hill. Like an ocean, she heard him say, listening from the dark of the stairs, closing her eyes to imagine waves of uniforms in blue. Sometimes Uncle Jack drank too much and would show up in the middle of the night with tears in his eyes, banging things and talking too loud. Sometimes he had something called incipient schizophrenia. But he was still her favourite uncle by a longshot because he always remembered her, always brought her things or sent presents in the mail – books, cassettes, calculators with foreign brand names – every year, never forgetting, wherever they moved. This year it was *Vivaldi, the Four Seasons* wrapped in red tissue, arriving just before they packed up again, just in time, "Happy Birthday Polly Jean, your first of many dozen" on an oversized card.

She fell in love with the concerto called "Winter," the music gorgeous and blooming in her headphones, curled and cocooning on the living room floor until her brother David stepped on her fingers and then the cassette case, cracking it, *You're stupid for leaving it there, who cares it was a piece of crap anyway.* And then a kick to the ribs for good measure.

Another bad sign, Polly Jean thought, one of a couple, if you looked straight into the face of the thing, if you were honest about it. Though not nearly as bad as the house not looking anything like the Polaroid her dad had waved around those months before, promising everything, not nearly as bad as her mom spending day after day in bed, empty and depressed by all the piled boxes again, lying there reading her exercise magazines. Not nearly as bad.

Sitting there in another new classroom with another new set of strangers, Polly Jean did not feel lucky at all. "She's one of the garbage kids," came the whisper stinging in her neck, but when Polly Jean turned around everyone was staring back, challenging.

So she shook her head at it, turned it away, tried to think of something else, but the only thing that came to mind was her enormous new pimple, a deep-cheek one high on the right side, just below her eye, pulsing and hurting.

"Well look at you," she had said to the mirror that morning.

Mrs. Lester sounded kind enough, calling Polly Jean's name smoothly and clearly against the muffled squawking, the mock parrot noises from the back of the classroom. But when she turned around she was old and severe, and she had that look which made sudden silence. "Do you like the news, Polly Jean?" she asked, eyebrows raised, chalk poised at the board under the heading CURRENT EVENT ASSIGNMENTS.

"Uh, I like seeing other places in the world," Polly Jean answered. Her lips wouldn't work right, seemed all tight in the corners. "Like on television, places like Africa or China."

But Mrs. Lester wasn't listening, was already writing her name beside an assignment. "How about Western Canada, then?" she asked.

"Okay," said Polly Jean weakly, her mind squeezing. She looked down at her hands, at her fingers splayed out before her. "Why do I always get the lame assignments?" she sighed in her little prayer voice, a little too loud.

"Maybe because you're a loser?" offered a flat-faced kid in the next row, the whisper hissing through a mess of metal in his mouth, and the room squeaked with nervous, farting laughter until Mrs. Lester turned around again.

Polly Jean's God dropped towns all over the place, loved playing *TOY TOWNS* on his prairie floor, tossing them down in tumbling little piles. Obviously there was a basic set-up but God always tinkered with the details, you could rely on that, and even the standard pieces – railway tracks, elevator, school, store, church, hardware, bank, post office, garage – were never exactly the same. Sometimes you'd even get multiples of things, especially churches. And then of course all the houses where people actually lived could be wildly dissimilar. Walking home from school that day Polly Jean worked on her mental notes, tried to take the town in, be observant, but the sun shimmered around too much, its light dissipated and seamless with the white of the snow, draining the place out, making everything washy and obscure. And it was warm for that time of year; her toque itched against her scalp, her body felt lazy and slack.

As an experiment, she wanted to walk a straight line from the school to her house, from one end of town to the other. Shortest distance between two points, at least worth a try. Maybe it was a mile. She passed along the long lane behind the seniors' housing, looking at the little garden sheds seep and sag in the identical backyard plots. Across the road the grain elevator loomed ahead, guarding the railway tracks that cut the town in two. There was a path leading to a space between the service sheds, and she followed it.

Railway tracks were always built up in small towns, always made you climb. Between the buildings the sun disappeared, the earth dipped, the gloom pressed in, air cool and close on her face. She was startled to find someone there, leaning against the building supports, smoking a cigarette. A boyish face looked up at her, scowling. Oh hullo, Polly Jean thought. It was Ian O'Hagan.

"What're ya doing there?" he called.

"I'm just going home," she called back, her voice thick.

Ian O'Hagan was the kind of kid that everyone knew right away. He sat at the back of her sixth grade class, trading punches with the Miller twins and flicking lit matches at open collars. Ian O'Hagan was the kind of kid who said that he didn't need school because he was going to take over his dad's farm anyway.

Polly Jean straightened her back and took a few steps forward. Ian O'Hagan's short black hair stood up in spikes, embalmed with gel. His leather jacket – from some hockey team, number eleven, left wing – was two sizes too big. In the half-light it seemed like his green eyes were burning.

"So? Keep going then," he said, like he was talking to a child.

Polly Jean tried to smile at him, but her mouth felt like a smear. "My name is Polly Jean," she said. "I'm in your class."

"Yeah, I know," he said, watching smoke hang in the air. "You're one of the new garbage man's kids."

Polly Jean straightened her glasses. The tiny screw for the left arm was loose again. "Actually, he's the new town man," she said, trying not to sound like she was correcting him. "He does a lot more than just the garbage."

Ian O'Hagan frowned at her. "How many of you kids are there anyway?"

"Seven, me and my six brothers," Polly Jean answered quickly. It was a memorized line.

"Yeah, my dad says poor people always have too many kids."

Polly Jean pretended not to hear that. She was standing still just a few feet away from him now. "So, you got Africa as your current events assignment?" she asked.

He blew air through his lips, made a dismissive sound. "Yeah, I guess, whatever."

"That's not so bad," Polly Jean offered, and then, the words just popping out of her mouth, "I could help you with that. If you wanted me to."

Ian O'Hagan snorted. "Yeah, and maybe you could just do the whole thing for me."

"Okay," Polly Jean said, and walked past him before he could say anything. "See you Monday," she called, but didn't dare look.

Her brothers were in the basement, torturing each other with pennies and a deck of cards, and her father was out again, a restless soul her mother said, a useless soul, while the door to the back bedroom remained silent and closed. And for once this was all good, because it gave Polly Jean run of the television for a few precious hours.

The documentary – on what her brothers dismissed as "the boring channel" – was called *Africa on the Edge*. It was fantastic. Images boiled away in front of her, seething montages that always ended with khaki-wearing, grim-faced reporters. She scrambled to scribble it all down, and in the end her notes offered up several sharp, shiny pieces – ragged mobs of war veterans singing death songs to white farmers in Zimbabwe, Islamic militants stealing in from the Algerian desert night to murder whole families, wild-eyed machine-gunning police charging around like cowboys in South Africa, flooding and misery without end in Mozambique – but the story that Polly Jean wrote about in detail was the assassination of the president of the Congo.

The president turned dictator. The massive bald head of the man, that weather-beaten picture plastered everywhere in the capital, a cult of personality they said, his country bleak and deranged, desperate, its colours lurid. Wheels within wheels and all of it chaos, the very heart of Africa turned in on itself they said, rebels and foreign armies seizing whole parts of the country, lawlessness the order of the day, blood diamonds and corruption and ancient tribal hatreds, piles of amputated limbs, the African World War they said. Killed by one of his own bodyguards. Betrayed. It played hot in Polly Jean's mind: dense, liquid imaginings of scheming and intrigue, evil forces in the jungle, the earth swallowing lives, God simply burning away against the African sun. She fell asleep there, in front of the television, until her dad came home and gave her a soft kick, complaining drunkenly to himself about a lousy pair of kings.

Hurry up, Polly Jean thought, pushing herself through the warm winter morning, rose-coloured light expanding all around, her heart big and full in her chest. Hurry up. She got there just before he did.

"Well hello," grinned the principal, key already in hand.

"Hullo," said Polly Jean.

"You're a keen one on a Monday morning," he remarked, working the heavy lock. His wet hair, combed straight back in severe lines, gave off little tuffs of steam. Staring up at his silhouette, he looked like a demon.

"Sometimes," Polly Jean replied, showing her teeth.

Inside the principal flicked a switch and the lights stuttered to electric attention down the length of the hallway, one by one by one. They walked to her classroom. "Mrs. Lester should be in any minute. You're okay here for now?" he asked, going to leave.

Polly Jean showed her teeth again. "I've got a book to read."

She unpacked her bag, counted to thirty, listened for footsteps. Nothing. Gently so gently she placed the folder on Ian O'Hagan's seat. Polly Jean felt sorry, looking at it now, how old and overused it was, the edges of the red cover rough and peeling. The inside, however, was very clean; after three drafts and half a pad of David's good paper Polly Jean was sure of that, had felt so sure as she typed it, one key at a time, each letter singing to her, the unerring roundness of her o's, the pure, true shape of her n's, all Sunday afternoon in rapture, until she had two perfect pages.

Rocking in her seat while she waited, her skin like voltage, and then she looked up, and then she looked up at the board and saw the words there, *Western Canada – Polly Jean*, and the shock knocked her mind flat with panic.

They stood there together before him, staring at the blood-hot spectacle of the thing, at this pure theatre of rage, the spittle foaming in the corner of the principal's mouth. If only steam would come out of his nostrils, Polly Jean thought. Then he would be perfect.

Whack went the yardstick against the top of the massive desk. *Whack whack whack* went the yardstick, like he was getting a feel for it. *WHACK* it made you start, made your eyes pinch and dart around, that was half of it Polly Jean guessed, at least half, and then she noticed the two heavy stones on top of the piles of paper, and *whack* she thought, oh I see, imagining an earlier episode, the furious sheets flying everywhere.

"So what we have here," pronounced the principal, *whack*, "is a cheater," *whack*, "and an idler." And then a lesser *whack* this time, followed by little more than a *sshtap*, the valley in his symphony of whacking. He stood there for a moment, face flushed and shoulders rounded, and stared hard at nothing. He took up the red folder in his free hand and regarded Ian O'Hagan with heavy, tired eyes. "For God's sake, boy," he implored, shaking the thing at him, blurring it in the air. "For God's sake, if you're going to plagiarize, at least have the decency and common sense to make the thing believable. Now what magazine did you copy this from?"

"I didn't," Ian O'Hagan shrugged.

WHACK! "Don't lie to me, boy! Where did you get it from?" He was roaring now, horrible breath blasting away.

Ian O'Hagan swayed back, gestured with his head. "*She* did it," he said, still just that tiny bit cocky. "*She* wrote it. I didn't even ask her. She *wanted* to do it."

The principal's face fell down at the sides. His voice was very cold. "There's nothing I find more distasteful than a liar, boy."

"It's true," Ian O'Hagan insisted, straightening himself like a defendant in the box. "It's true, I swear."

The principal regarded Polly Jean with somewhat more sympathy. "You've found yourself in some very bad company, young lady. What do you have to say about all this?"

The statement was true and the question was fair – she had to admit that – yet how appalling the truth looked, at a quarter after ten in the morning, the thin red hand struggling with the seconds.

"Well?"

Polly Jean's breath piled and pushed at her. Oh I know, she thought, this feeling, all of it swelling up inside of her now, this thing that just went on and on, wanting to keep her forever, and she just had to get through, through and through and then finally out, there would be that day, she was sure of that, and from far away there might still be flashes of this and all the rest on the distant horizon, when she would make little noises to herself, the kind that only memory, stealing in behind daydreams, can squeeze out of you. But then it would be only that.

"Yes, it's true," she said, trying to look small, letting the words quiver. "Except he forced me to, he threatened me, told me he would break my nose if I didn't, and I'm new here and I don't know anyone and I was scared."

WHACK went the yardstick, splinters spinning out like pieces of a bomb and all courage blown away, tears everywhere, the principal had to leave the room just to compose himself, throw water against his forehead, trying to put his face back together again in the bathroom mirror, and when he came back Ian O'Hagan was still crying and Polly Jean was gone.

... which is how she came to me. How we found each other. She was walking down the shoulder of the old highway. That's a gift, I said to myself. So I took it.

Now Mr. Carey, I know you and your prosecutor's mind are not going to be happy with the little narrative I've written here, you're going to say this isn't keeping with our agreement (un-holy as we both know it is), and there is a part of me that can see what you mean, but I have to tell you, Mr. Carey, that I am not trying to cheat you, and this really is her story, believe me she had lots of time to tell me, and the one part that you will never understand is that this was always about the stories anyway, especially the ones I keep for myself.

Darryl Joel Berger grew up in the village of Perdue, Saskatchewan, along with six siblings. He delivered newspapers throughout highschool. He attended the University of Saskatchewan while working summers at a psychiatric hospital in North Battleford, Saskatchewan. He graduated with a BA in Political Science and later, with a diploma in Graphic Design from Red River College in Winnipeg, Manitoba. He started writing stories to accompany illustrations submitted to magazines. His fiction has since been published in literary magazines across Canada and the United States. He is a winner of the David Adams Richards Prize, a finalist in the Commonwealth Short Story Competition, and a finalist in the Malahat Review's Novella Prize. He lives with his wife Christina and daughter Oona in Kingston, Ontario. You can follow his work at www.red-handed.blogspot.com.